Aric McBay

INVERSION

With the Black Dawn series we honor anarchist traditions and follow the great Octavia E. Butler's legacy, Black Dawn seeks to explore themes that do not reinforce dependency on oppressive forces (the state, police, capitalism, elected officials) and will generally express the values of antiracism, feminism, anticolonialism, and anticapitalism. With its natural creation of alternate universes and world-building, speculative fiction acts as a perfect tool for imagining how to bring forth a just and free world. The stories published here center queerness, Blackness, antifascism, and celebrate voices previously disenfranchised, all who are essential in establishing a society in which no one is oppressed or exploited. Welcome, friends, to Black Dawn!

BLACK DAWN SERIES #5

SANINA L. CLARK, SERIES EDITOR

ISBN 9781849355049
E-ISBN 9781849355056
LCCN: 2023935630

AK Press
370 Ryan Ave. #100
Chico, CA 95973
www.akpress.org

AK Press
33 Tower Street
Edinburgh, Scotland EH6 7BN
akuk.com

Cover art by Bob Kayganich, www.bobkayganich.com
Cover design and logo by T. L. Simons, tlsimons.com
Printed in the USA

To the practical utopians.

INVERSION

Chapter I

One Day in a Beautiful World

Char of the Ami

I was twenty-two when my grandfather went into the flamewall.

He had circled the world 348 times—a good age for anyone—and he was simply tired. He'd had enough of walking and his joints ached no matter how much milkroot he ate.

Grandfather declared this one afternoon, while we were burying broken equipment and old books. We held the ceremony that night, our relatives leaving one by one as they said goodbye. The next morning as the sun rose from the East Pole, my grandfather strode through the autumn leaves and into the flames, looking back only once with his bright green eyes.

He went in humming the steam-bending song, so that as a child in the next life, he might show aptitude for box-making or boat-building. Within the heat shimmer, his body seemed to come apart—not burning but dissolving like a wisp of smoke in a strong breeze.

The Winter People will find a green-eyed baby in one of their cradles when the flames recede.

My grandmother was the picture of equanimity; she had seen death, sudden and violent, at a young age. So, it was only ten minutes after my grandfather's passing when she stood with clear eyes, hugged Uncle Tycho, and beckoned to me. "Char, my granddaughter," she said. "Let's go meet the others in spring."

I wiped the tears from my cheeks and wheeled over a tricycle, which had room for two. She sat beside me in the broad and comfortable seat. We pedaled slowly, away from the wall of flame that had gained on us by twenty feet while we'd watched it.

We left behind a dozen supply caches (already engulfed in flame), a few comrades who would follow shortly, and my grandmother's partner of fifty years.

It was autumn near the flame front, of course. The grass between the trees was yellow and lay close to the ground. The foliage on the oaks and maples above was orange and red and yellow. Fallen leaves on the path crunched beneath our wheels and stirred up in our wake.

We followed a coastal path that wound its way between the seashore on our left and intermittent patches of forest and prairie on our right. In the distant grasslands I spotted a herd of bison.

The scents varied as we traveled: the salt of the ocean, the smell of dew in grass, and flowers alongside the path. The breeze dried the last tears from my cheeks.

As we rode, the leaves changed—growing greener, fuller. The grass became verdant and upright.

Summer was my favorite season. On the air I could smell fresh apples; we passed bushes and shrubs weighted down by fragrant berries. We waved at a group of people—other Ami—in their circle of wagons around a campfire. A bit further, we passed a young couple building a cradle from stones and branches. When we reached early summer, I caught a glimpse of a faun through the underbrush. Songbirds frolicked above, their tunes mingling with the whir of the tricycle wheels.

Finally, after an hour or so of quiet travel, we reached spring. I glanced over to see my grandmother had closed her eyes, smiling slightly as the wind of our passage swept over her creased face and tousled her white hair.

As we passed into early spring, leaves receded into their buds. Blossoming flowers disappeared. The green grass shortened, brightened, and then vanished under a fine layer of ash.

I slowed to a stop as we reached the very edge of spring, and we disembarked. Children ran back and forth, searching for caches, their feet wrapped in thick leather to protect them from the latent heat of the flames just passed.

The spring flame front ahead was receding slowly away from us. The faithful flames consumed, but they also renewed.

A cradle had emerged from the fires. My cousin Theo rushed to it with excitement, but it was empty, as they all had been for months. Some Ami had begun to grumble that the Spring People had grown selfish.

Nearby, a few children laughed with excitement; they'd found the edge of a metal canister protruding from the ash, just where the map had said it would be. They waved for an adult and Theo approached with thick gloves and a shovel to dig it out.

The lid had my grandmother's name etched into the top. Theo brought it to her and cracked open the lid. She reached inside and drew out a book—something thick and spiral-bound—still warm from the heat of the fires.

My grandmother regarded it skeptically and then gazed up across the world toward the rising sun.

....

The world is made of circles; you can see it at a glance.

From the Ami path, near the West Pole, I could raise my head eastward and see nearly the entire universe. From within the deep rainforest or the misty mountain valleys one might imagine the universe was any shape at all, even a vast expanse like in the days of old. But on a sunny day near the poles, one can see our universe exactly as it is: a hollow sphere. Its surface—continents and oceans, islands and coral reefs—all divided into three sections by three lines of flame that run from pole to pole.

The inexorable fires sweep slowly around the world like the hands of a clock, or so Uncle Tycho was fond of saying. He had a collection of watches and clocks he repaired with tiny tools. It was slow and tedious work that attracted no apprentices. We could all tell what time it was by the position of the sun. And what use was it to measure every second if you spent them staring into the minuscule gears of malfunctioning antiques from an age when the universe itself was broken?

The three sections of the world had their usual three seasons, visible in triplicate. As each flamewall progressed, it left spring behind it. Plants and trees matured into summer, birds laid eggs and hatched them, trees blossomed and set fruit. Then, as if exhausted by their efforts, the grasses would turn yellow, the trees would turn orange, and the autumn flamewall would arrive to begin the cycle again.

One month. That's how long a given tree or patch of grass had in which to do whatever it wanted to do before it would be renewed.

At the forested equator, the distance the flamewalls traveled in the span of a month was enormous. But here, near the pole, spring and fall were less than a day's walk apart.

....

My grandmother and I had made that journey swiftly by trike. As my grandmother inspected the book that had been pulled from the cache in the ground, my Aunt Scarlet approached. She gave my grandmother a hug, then turned to me. "Char, can you find me some softleaf today? Victor has a sore ankle."

I shook my head. "No time for herbs. I'm teaching with Uncle Tycho today. World lessons for the summer kids."

"Of course!" she said, remembering. My grandfather's passing had disrupted the usual schedule. I trained with her in herbalism and bike repair several times a week, but this was my day with Uncle Tycho.

Like many people in their early twenties, I had ample freedom to dabble. I could apprentice in a dozen crafts each month. By the time I'm twenty-five, though, I'll have walked a hundred laps of the world and the older Ami will start asking when I might choose a specialty—both to serve the community and to relieve an elder of some duties.

In the meantime, I could focus on my studies. I could get my hands greasy as a bicycle mechanic. And I could work to memorize each of the hundred different medicinal herbs on our circuit, their locations and active ingredients: the anti-inflammatories in softleaf, the analgesic sedatives in milkroot, the mélange of empathogens and cannabinoids in a friendship tea made from bitter licorice.

Saying farewell, I left Scarlet and my grandmother in spring and rode back toward summer. I found Tycho's blue wagon in a fruit grove that overlooked the Western Sea. He wasn't there—still making his way back from my grandfather's autumn ceremony—but the walls of his wagon were covered in his favorite things: clocks, books, a few telescopes, and flame-crafted lenses and other contraptions.

My stomach was growling. I went to the closest buffet tree; some of its branches bore ripe pears, others apples, still others avocados, and I picked one of each for breakfast. Then I sat in the lush grass at the edge of the orchard and gazed out over the ocean.

There were dark sandy beaches to the north. But here the coast was flat and rocky, with long shelves of granite broken up by tidal pools and little inlets. I always felt relaxed by the sea, and I needed a moment of quiet after the emotional intensity of my grandfather's passing. The sound of the waves and the distant polar gyre were gentle whispers, as if the sea were hushing herself. "Shhhhhh . . ." The fresh breeze coming up from the shore was infused with the scent of low tide, a briny mélange of fish and drying seaweed. My stomach growled as I ate.

The Western Sea before me was roughly circular, its surface gently dished to match the spherical contours of the universe. I felt as if I were sitting on the edge of an enormous bowl; not a bowl *containing* water, but a bowl *made* of water. The sea was speckled with distant polar islands of different colors—the Onyx Isle, the Gray Whale, the Red Rock—which encircled its whirling center. I breathed in deeply and closed my eyes, letting the gentle wind caress my face. My cheeks were tickled by a few free strands of hair that had come loose from my braid.

By the time I had finished eating, I could hear the laughter of children making their way across the orchard. With impeccable timing, as usual, Uncle Tycho pulled up on his bicycle, ready to begin the day's lesson. He greeted me as always, "Char, my favorite niece!" I was his only niece. He hugged me and turned to the children.

"Good morning, kids!" he said. "Let's head down to the shore. Time to learn about the world."

....

"The universe," Uncle Tycho told the kids in hushed tones, "used to be inside-out." His diminutive audience—gathered around a tidal pool on the rocky shore—leaned forward to hear him over the sound of the waves.

"This is too scary for the little children," he said, still speaking in a dramatic stage whisper, "but *you* are old enough to know." Violet, a five-year-old sitting beside me, leaned toward him, her eyes wide.

"The world before ours—the cosmos, they called it—was inside-out," Tycho continued. "The universe was not a cozy orb enclosing us like a cradle. It was a vast expanse of empty vacuum." He paused, turning to Violet. "That means you couldn't breathe in it!

"The sun was not our sweet small droplet of warm light," Tycho said, gesturing up, "which moves each day from pole to pole like a faithful friend. It was a huge and ragged thing that grew redder and angrier by the day, boiling the seas as it lashed out with angry arms." Violet leaned toward me and clutched my knee.

"When the universe was inside-out, the stars were not our neighbors," Tycho continued. "They did not undulate gently above our campfires at night. They were distant beyond understanding; even their faintest flicker of light took many lifetimes to reach us."

"Wait," interrupted Violet, "if they were so far away, how did they clean our air?" She sounded genuinely worried about it, so I put a gentle hand on her back.

"They didn't!" Tycho replied, switching from a whisper to a booming declaration. "They couldn't. They weren't the little companions we are used to but flaming monsters bigger than this entire world! And yet, they were so incredibly distant that we could see just a pinprick of light. If we were lucky, that is. For sometimes the stars themselves would explode without warning and instead of cleaning our air, they would send bursts of light so bright that it burned the air itself away!"

I glanced around the circle. The children were rapt, the younger ones swept up in the storytelling while the older children were clearly trying to imagine how the ancient cosmos would have appeared. I did the same, gazing up and imagining that instead of a sphere of blue-tinged continents overhead, were we surrounded only by an empty void, a vast blankness broken only by hostile stars. The idea made me shiver. That was why we told these stories in daytime; telling children these things in the dark would only give them nightmares.

"But the biggest danger wasn't the sun," Uncle Tycho said, nudging me. "Isn't that right?"

"That's right," I said, joining in. "A harsh universe made harsh people. Some of them were cruel. Instead of letting us go our own way, they chased our ancestors from place to place. Instead of taking care of *themselves*, they made us work for them. Instead of sharing, they took everything for themselves. They hated anyone different, and in the end, they ruined the land and even the stars themselves."

"But our ancestors were wise and smart," Tycho said. "They wanted us to be safe, to live as we saw fit. So, they brought us here to Germinal, where we would be protected. Just like the creatures in this pool." Finally, he gestured to the tidal pool, and the children leaned forward to peer into it.

The pool was crowded with life. Anemones with waving rainbow tendrils lined the ledges inside. Little crabs crawled back and forth in search of snails. There were even a few sea urchins and some five-limbed handfish.

Violet reached in to pet the closest handfish, and the nearby anemones puckered shut at the passage of her shadow.

"It's so much smaller than the ocean," said Violet. "Do they have enough to eat?"

"They do," said Tycho. "Because they all *share* the pool. It's their commons. And because every day the tides rise and fall to bring new water and food."

"It's like the flamewalls," I added, "that keep the land fresh and new."

"But what if a shark gets in and tries to eat them all?" asked Violet.

Tycho was gentle. "A shark can't fit in the pool, Violet, even at high tide."

"But what if a shark gets in to eat *us*?" she insisted. "In *our* pool."

"The tidal pool is just a metaphor, darling," Tycho said. "We've been here close to a thousand years. There are no sharks to bother us."

....

By mid-morning our seaside lesson had progressed into simple play. Children were going from pool to pool, searching for the most interesting things before the tide came back in.

Violet was obsessed with handfish. She liked to reach into the pools and gently pry them loose, turning them over and staring at their undersides and the hundreds of tiny tube-feet they used to move around. Often, she would bring them to me or to Tycho. Now she rushed over to us. "This handfish is broken!" she exclaimed, proffering her latest find.

"Technically, they aren't fish," Tycho explained as he accepted it. "They're invertebrates, similar to sea urchins." He flipped it over and pointed to the mouth at its center, where the five arms met. "See, no head. Just a mouth."

She poked the mouth gently.

"They eat clams by prying open their shells first," I told her. "Then they vomit their entire stomach inside the clam's shell so they can dissolve its flesh and slurp up the juices."

"Whoa!" Violet answered softly, with a child's mingled awe and horror.

"But you're right that this one was injured," Tycho said. One of the five arms was much smaller and shorter than the others. "Maybe an arm got eaten. Did you know that handfish can grow back their body parts? They could regenerate that way even when the universe was still inside-out, before the flamewalls."

"Oooh," she said, touching the stubby arm.

"Put them back so they don't dry out," Tycho said, and Violet did.

Further down the rocky shore, the other children had

found a small dome of translucent jelly, trailing a few feet of tentacles.

"Careful!" I said. "The tentacles of a starfish can sting you. It's how they catch their prey." One of the older kids poked the gelatinous remnants with a stick, keeping a safe distance.

"When they are alive," Tycho explained, "starfish glow faintly, just like real stars. Hence the name."

"Hello!" a voice called from the orchard above. It was my grandmother carrying a covered basket. Time for lunch.

We herded the children back to the shade of the fruit trees near Tycho's wagon. Grandmother had brought potato biscuits and fried fish.

"Thanks for the fish, Red Grandma!" said Violet.

"Don't thank *me* for the fish!" she said. "Thank the Ternfolk and the Western Sea."

The children stood obediently and bowed toward the ocean. In the distance, where the sea curved up toward the whirling pole, we could spot little white sails.

"Thank you, Ternfolk!" the children said in unison. "Thank you, Western Sea!"

As the children settled down with their food, Tycho retrieved a stool from his wagon and offered it to Grandmother. She found a place to sit where all the children could see her.

"Alright, children," she began. "I'm going to tell you something very important. Something so important our lives here in Germinal depend on it."

The children stared attentively, silent except for the sounds of their chewing.

"Every part of something contains a memory of the whole," she said.

"We know!" Violet said cheerfully.

"Oh, you do!" Grandmother smiled, indulgently surprised at the interruption. "How do you know that?"

"Because," Violet enthused, "because, because, because when you bury a broken bicycle gear in a cache it comes back fixed!"

"Only because of the flamewall," said Aldebrand, an older child.

"That's true," said Grandmother. "The gear remembers what it was supposed to be like, and the flamewall renews it. What else?"

"Medicine!" another child said. "If you break aspirin pills in half and bury them in a cache, they come back full of twice as many."

"Exactly," said Grandmother encouragingly. "Or, for aspirin, we could boil a tea from sea willow. What else?"

"Trees!" exclaimed the next child. "If a branch breaks in a storm, the flamewall will fix it. Or, if you want a pear tree to have apple fruit, you can cut a branch off from an apple tree and stick it on the pear tree before the flamewall comes!"

"That's called flame-grafting," Grandmother agreed.

"Handfish!" yelled Violet. "If they're missing an arm."

Grandmother looked to Tycho, who said, "Handfish grow their own arms back, hon."

"That's right," said Grandmother. "The flamewalls don't heal animals. If an animal goes into the flamewall, it comes out as a new, different animal on the other side."

"Or a new, different human," I said.

....

Once we had finished our biscuits and fish, Uncle Tycho led the kids in a rousing game of "find the cache." They ran around the orchard, searching for caches that had started to poke up above the surface of the soil. It was much easier to do in spring—before the grass began to grow—but it kept the kids engaged and it was a good skill to be able to find caches anywhere.

While they were occupied, I took a moment to check in with my grandmother. "How are you doing?" I asked.

She offered me a complicated smile. "I'm sad that he's gone," she said, "and tired from staying up late talking to him. Happy that he's going to the next life after he'd grown so exhausted here. But missing him already." Tears came to my eyes just from listening to her. She reached out to lay a warm hand on my cheek. "It's easier when you get to my age. I've seen many come and go. On balance it's a joy, not a sorrow, but that doesn't mean it's always easy."

"Are you sure you don't want to *rest* today?" I asked.

"I can rest when I please," she answered. "Right now, I want to spend time with you and Tycho and the children and all of the Ami." I nodded and pulled her in for a hug. My grandmother always put the community first; it was why she was so respected in her role as conciliator. Her ability to resolve argument and forge agreement between conflicting groups was legendary. I aspired to do the same work someday, once I'd accrued enough wisdom. Even my own father—her son after Tycho—had pursued a career of building bridges between the people of Germinal, though with the more ambitious aim of cultural unification.

"I'm sorry," I said, "that my parents aren't here for this."

"They've chosen their own path," she answered, still holding me close. "Let's hope that they get what they want from their Tapestry mission in the desert."

Tycho and the children called to us, and we walked over to see what they had found. They had used their child-sized trowels to dig up half a dozen caches and piled them in the shade of a massive oak. Its curving branches loomed over us like the bulk of the world itself.

"And what did you find?" Grandmother asked.

In tumultuous sequence, the children showed her the contents of each clay cylinder. A metal canteen, embossed with an abstract pattern like flowing water. Two pairs of bright green sandals. A dozen sets of silver cutlery jammed into a single container. A strong narrow rope, like the kind the Ternfolk used to raise their sails. A handful of carbon fiber pulleys for hunting crossbows. And a large, flat book, rolled up and bound with twine so it would fit in the cylindrical cache.

"Oh, these are very beautiful!" she said, complimenting each item in turn. "Good job for finding them! Is there anything here you want to keep?"

Hubbub followed as the children discussed—passing around the too-big green sandals to try on, inspecting the artistic pattern on the canteen. In short order, though without any clear process, it was decided that the rope would be offered to the Ternfolk, the pulleys to the Grasslanders, and that Aldebrand would keep the canteen since his own had sprung a leak after being dropped too many times.

The only dispute was over the destiny of the book, which Violet clung to and seemed unwilling to part with.

Books were an exception to the usual "finders, keepers" rule. Since my childhood, Grandmother and Tycho had been trying to reassemble scraps of old manuals. On one occasion Grandmother had found enough pages of one book that she glued them together at the spine and buried them in a cache, hoping the flamewall would fill in the gaps. She finally dug it up, one lap later, to find a complete volume—*The Eternal Flame Revisited:*

Prolonging Waveform Collapse for Ecological Rejuvenation—but the inside was nonsense. The process hadn't worked, clearly. It was full of nonsense words like "asido," "oaiasofi," and "chromodynamics," so she had merely thrown it on the ground and left it there.

"Violet," said Tycho. "If you find pages, you should always offer them to Red Grandma first."

There was a long pause as Violet frowned intensely, clutching the book. I was about to step in when Violet capitulated, exhaling slowly and passing the book over to Grandmother. Grandma untied the twine, unrolled and inspected the pages. It wasn't a manual. Just a comic book of the kind that had been passed in and out of caches for centuries. Each time it went through the flamewall, it came out slightly different. This meant that the old comics were full of long strings of seemingly nonsensical dialogue and scenes rendered in odd color combinations, but the children found them entertaining. After flipping through it, Grandmother passed it back to Violet, who grinned broadly.

Violet opened the comic book again and stared at the text thoughtfully. "Do you think the Spring People would write a message in a cache for us?" she asked.

"No," Tycho said at once. "It's not allowed to read messages from the Spring People or to send them to the Winter People. They're too different from us."

"But why?" Violet asked.

"Our peoples have been separate since the beginning of Germinal," Tycho said. "Separate goals and values," he added. "The Spring People are prideful, aggressive. And the Winter People more . . . introspective. You'll understand when you're older."

There were other reasons, of course, concepts too mature for Violet, who didn't really grasp Tycho's simplified version. But this was an old rule among the Ami and a firm one. Perhaps in some avant-garde desert polity people wrote messages back and forth beneath the flamewall every day. But here the matter was not up for debate. Grandmother continued with the lesson.

"And what are we going to put *back* into the caches when we bury them again?" Grandmother asked. Aldebrand offered his old canteen at once. The other children were not as forthcoming. They loved *finding* caches more than filling them, but children needed to learn the lesson of reciprocity and that meant practicing it.

Grandmother offered a folding pocketknife with a broken hinge, even though I was sure that Tycho could have fixed it without sending it through the flamewall. I gave a leaky innertube from my tricycle. The silverware and green sandals went back into the caches they'd come from. That left only one empty cache—the clay cylinder that had contained the comic book Violet now held.

She was busy flipping through the pages and took a while to realize we were all watching her. "But I don't have anything to give!" she said, clearly worried she might have to return her book.

Tycho stepped in, obligingly, with set of cracked lenses he had in his wagon.

Tycho, Aldebrand, and I pulled the trowels from our belts to re-bury the caches. Violet and the other youngsters "assisted" the process by pointing out where they thought we should dig the holes and how deep.

"Dig more!" demanded Violet, after I had already excavated a hole two feet deep. "More deep! Dig to the bottom!"

"No!" Grandmother said, more sternly than even I expected. Then, a bit more softly, she added, "You should never dig too deep."

She stared off to the distance for a moment, lost in thought, and Tycho spoke up. "That would be dangerous, Violet. And we have to keep each other safe." He turned to the group of children. "Who keeps us safe?"

"We keep us safe!" the children replied in unison. I mouthed it along with them.

"And what do you do," Tycho prompted, "if you see someone in danger?"

Their responses were more varied, "Warn them!" "Help them!" "Step up!" "Shout 'Danger!'" But they all boiled down to the same ethos: responsibility and action.

It was a lesson the Ami had learned the hard way.

....

When my grandmother was a child, something terrible happened.

She'd had a beautiful older brother named Indigo with rare purple eyes. The two had been inseparable and voraciously curious.

All children are curious about the flamewall. That's natural. Who wouldn't be curious about the most powerful phenomenon in our world?

Children slake their thirst for knowledge through experiments. What happens if we bury a cache with a broken cup? In a couple of months, we can dig it up, brand new. What if we bury a cup without a clay container? It burns up to nothing. If you bury something deep enough, can it escape the flamewall? Nobody has ever done it.

The two children had seen that birds who flew very high could pass over the flamewall untouched, moving freely to the Spring People or the Winter People. So, they asked the next logical question: could you go *under* the flamewall?

They dug many holes, as deeply as they could, burying caches of cracked bowls as tests. Near the Amber Moon they dug three feet before hitting bedrock. On a sandy beach they made it five feet before their hole flooded from the bottom. In the forest thick roots slowed them so much that they had only made it seven feet deep by the time autumn and the flamewall approached. The following lap, once spring had come, they dug up those caches and found their bowls, good as new, reformed by flame.

Clearly, the flamewall reached far into the ground.

Other children would have given up early when faced with so much work and so little reward. My grandmother and her brother persisted, even though the older children teased them for their fruitless work.

In summer, they finally found a spot in a copse of trees on the edge of the grassland where the soil was soft. They dug for two weeks. After the hole had gotten deep enough that they couldn't jump out of it, they built a ladder so they could keep extending their vertical shaft into the ground. Indigo hung a pulley from a strong branch overhead so they could use a bucket to lift dirt from the bottom.

When autumn came, their vertical shaft was twelve feet deep. They *could* have buried a cache and been done with it. But then they would have had to refill the hole and dig it again in spring.

My little grandmother came up with the clever idea: why not dig a tunnel going crosswise, traveling horizontally in the direction of the flamewall? Then when the flamewall arrived, they could watch with their own eyes to see if extended down through the soil.

They were children. They didn't know any better.

It's a miracle, in a way, that the soft soil didn't collapse on them as they dug their tunnel, day after day. It's a tragedy that the adults, seeing them wash dirt out of their hair each afternoon, didn't intervene.

When the autumn flamewall finally arrived, they sat at the bottom of the ladder where the two passages met, staring down the twenty-foot length of their tunnel as the flamewall marched implacably forward. The flames appeared at the end of the tunnel, slowly at first and then quickly, rushing toward them.

My grandmother made it out. Her brother didn't.

People consoled each other in the usual way. "He's with the Winter People now." But in the eighty years since, no child with purple eyes has been born to the Ami. I think my grandmother still misses him.

I still see a glimpse of fear in her eyes when the children want to dig deep. It's the only time she is brusque or stern. Now, if Ami children ask how deep the flamewall goes, adults just say, "It goes all the way down."

....

The night before everything changed, the Grasslanders brought us bison for dinner.

The children had all washed up after digging up the caches. Four Grasslanders arrived on their tandem bicycles, fierce and proud with bundles of fresh meat wrapped in bison skin. The children offered the crossbow pulleys they had dug from the cache—not an exchange, just a mutual gift—and Tycho offered a set of binoculars he had repaired. The Grasslanders left with smiles on their faces.

A few dozen Ami converged, and we cooked the meat over an enormous campfire along with fresh summer vegetables. More Ami came, attracted by the smell of roasting meat and the smoke wafting from the fire.

Ignatius—part of the Tapestry tradition who, like my parents, had spent time in nearly every community from pole to pole—performed a lengthy poem that alternated among the Ami, Tern, and Grasslander dialects, celebrating the sacrifices of each plant and animal who had given their lives for us to eat.

When the food was almost ready, the children began their proclamations of gratitude. They gave thanks to the sun and the soil. To the Grasslanders and the Ternfolk and all the other Habitants. To the stars in the sky and the moons on the ground. To each kind of vegetable we were eating and to the bison who had given their lives.

I was famished after the day's exertions and devoured my dinner in the company of my family.

But Violet, instead of finishing her bison and carrots, was flopping around on the grass with her arms and legs outstretched like a handfish.

"What are you doing, my love?" Grandmother asked.

"I'm a hunter!" Violet answered.

"Maybe you should hunt your dinner."

"You're my dinner!" Violet roared in reply. She reached one arm toward Grandmother, wiggling her fingers as if catching an underwater scent. Then she stepped out of character for a moment to whisper, "I'm a handfish and you're a clam." Grandmother nodded her assent and wisely set her bowl a safe distance away.

Violet flopped closer to Grandmother and started inching one arm up her body. "I'm going to eat you!"

Grandmother pulled her hands together in front of her, "I'm a clam and you can't get through my shell!"

Violet climbed onto her lap, abandoning the posture of a

handfish, and tried to pry her hands apart. "I'm too strong," she shouted, "your shell can't stop me!"

After a few moments of gentle resistance, Grandmother allowed Violet to get past her shell and fell backward slowly onto the grass with her. Violet pantomimed digestion, an act she accompanied with very true-to-life puking sounds.

"Gross, Violet!" said Cousin Theo. "We're trying to eat!"

"I'm dissolving you!" Violet giggled. "I'm slurping you out of your shell!"

It was such a playful and innocent moment. A delightful, precious interlude.

Only later would I think of it again in fear.

....

Near the poles at sunset, when the wind was calm, you could hear the sun faintly as it passed. A deep, wordless hum that wandered up and down in pitch, like a lullaby sung by an old man who had lost his hearing.

The sun set as we finished our dinner, sinking into the Western Sea. The children recited the sunset prayer. And then, from the Eastern Pole, the stars emerged. They glowed brightly, their light reflecting off the flat rocky moons embedded in the land over our heads. The stars and the moons together made it just bright enough, once your eyes adjusted, not to trip in the dark when you walked through the grass at night.

We kept the campfire going, piled on dry branches to make it big and bright. In the great distance, above and beyond the flamewall, we could see a few flickering pinpricks of light from similar campfires in the lands of the Winter People. A thunderstorm was rolling over the lands of the Spring People, with flashes of lightning that we could see but not hear through thick clouds. The storm slid inexorably toward us, and we enjoyed our fire all the more knowing that rain was coming.

But our blazing fire made me think back on what Tycho had said about the stars *before*, when the universe was inside-out, how the old stars had been enormous spheres of deadly flame. I shivered, despite the warmth.

A gray haze accumulated in the sky above our campfire. One of the stars dipped down close to sweep the smoke from the air. We all watched in wonder as its luminous, undulating bell propelled it in slow circles above our heads. Its many trailing tendrils glowed dimly. The whole star was as wide across as my arm span and no longer than a minute's walk.

Our stars were cozy stars, their light cool and gentle and constant.

The thunderheads above the Spring People drifted gradually toward us, flashing silently. Once the storm crossed the spring flamewall, we could hear the growing rumble of thunder and took shelter to sleep in our wagons and tents.

....

That next morning, as always, the sun burst from the eastern sandstorm with vigor, buzzing like a beehive as it ascended from the desert. It climbed rapidly above the little villages of the desert polities, where dozens of different offshoot groups built experimental communities to test new social and economic ideas.

The dawn sky was calm; the rain had come and gone in the night. The storms had cleared so much humidity from the air that I could see all the way into the Spring People's lands.

But there I saw smoke. Several plumes of dark sooty smoke

emanating near their routes. Even with binoculars, it was too far to see what had happened. I knew that Tycho probably had something in his wagon that could magnify more strongly, but in the moment it just didn't seem important.

I assumed at the time the fires were caused by lightning strikes from the storm. There were big pines on the edge of the grasslands so thick with resin that they could go up like a torch after a lightning strike, even in the pouring rain.

We had camped close to the spring flamewall, so at dawn many of us ambled over to see what its passing might have left for us. I casually surveyed the ash for caches poking above the surface, even as the narrow tips of green grass were just starting to emerge.

I heard a scream a short distance away.

When it came again, I realized it was a scream of joy. I rushed toward the source to find Theo and his partner beside a cradle that had emerged from the flames overnight.

I approached to a respectful distance, joining a loose semi-circle of friendly spectators. Theo and his partner, Victor, who had already removed their shirts, lifted a baby gently from the cradle. It was asleep, quiescent, covered in the same thick milkpaste as all newborns.

They held the infant between their bodies until the child warmed, gently spreading the milkpaste onto their skin. Once the adults had absorbed it, they would begin to lactate so they could feed their hungry child.

After a few minutes the baby began to stir. The new parents laughed with joy, and we all smiled at the sight of it. "Their name will be Quang Duc," Victor announced. A hero's name.

My grandmother joined the semi-circle and then, at a gesture from Theo, approached. She offered a blanket to wrap the child, and Theo tucked the baby into it, gently passing the infant to her.

She was careful not to touch the milkpaste on the baby's skin—she had no interest in breast-feeding in her eighties—and she rocked the baby gently back and forth as she sang a song.

As she gazed at the infant, I caught just a glimpse of the child's bright purple eyes.

"Welcome back to the world," my grandmother whispered.

....

The entire day—the entire week—would have become a celebration if it hadn't been for what happened next.

Uncle Tycho, always watching the skies, spotted something high above. A balloon made of paper, wafting gently over the heat shimmer above the spring flamewall.

It must have floated up above the smoke, up where the pull of the ground was weak, and the air was thin and cold. Up near the stars.

It drifted down from the clouds that morning, landing on the softest of spring ashes. It had been made from paper, glued carefully around a cage of thin reeds. Beneath the balloon was a basket holding the burned-out stub of a candle, and a flat piece of metal into which someone had hastily scratched a single word.

"HELP."

Chapter 2

REPO

Char of the Ami

"This message is an affront," my grandmother declared. "How dare they?"

A handful of us stood around the deflated paper balloon, which was slumped sideways in the ash of the receding flamewall. The metal plate with the word "HELP" on it lay in the ash.

"Something must be terribly wrong," Aunt Scarlet replied, "for such a proud people to send it."

Uncle Tycho was listening without turning toward us but staring up and across the world at the plumes of smoke in the Spring People's third of the universe. "Exceptional," he agreed.

"There are reasons we don't send messages," Grandmother said, glancing in the direction of Theo and Victor holding the purple-eyed infant. "We shouldn't even be looking at this balloon."

It was taboo to send a message to the Spring or Winter People. It was taboo for us to receive one. It wasn't only the cultural difference. If we did communicate, it would be too tempting to reach out to lost loved ones among the Winter People or to demand children from the Spring People. Once someone has gone through the flamewall, they are a different person living a different life. We must be patient until, in future lives, we meet again.

"I'm going to get a telescope," Tycho said, grabbing his bicycle and riding back toward his wagon.

"We should call for a Convergence," Aunt Scarlet said, "to talk about what to do. Or at least consult the other Ami."

Ignatius, wearing his long Tapestry cloth like a multicolored poncho, joined us. "We cannot accept this message," Ignatius said firmly. "Or share it with others."

"See!" Grandmother said. "Even Tapestry agrees, and they usually want to talk to *everybody.*"

"If there are other balloons, we should destroy them," Ignatius said, scanning the sky as if another might drift in at any moment. "Furthermore—"

Before he could finish speaking, there was a sound like rumbling thunder. All around us, Ami looked up. Despite the deafening noise, there was barely a cloud on our side of the universe. The rumbling dulled but continued, as though echoing across distant mountains.

High up—*very* high, as though close to the sun—I could see something like a school of glinting silver fish in the sky. They moved toward us, not swimming but slowly falling.

Shielding my eyes from the sun, I watched the shapes move closer. They were not in fact fish but much larger things and fell toward the dry grasslands to the east. One by one they caught fire as they fell, belching dark smoke that trailed down instead of up.

The Ami around me gasped at the strange and frightening spectacle. The not-fish disappeared into their own smoke, leaving columns of gray that stretched down from the sky like the long fingers of a hand reaching to touch the yellow grassland.

The nearby rumbling grew, and then, as the smoke touched the grass, abruptly stopped.

"What are they?" I asked.

I looked to my grandmother, whose wide-open eyes were locked on the dark pillars of smoke, smoke that now drifted toward autumn in the gentle wind. At the point where each met the ground, I could see glinting metal. The not-fish hadn't burned up, at least not completely. They had landed like sparrows in the dry grass.

"They've started fires," my grandmother said. I saw her eyes had shifted from surprise to determination. It was true. Where the not-fish sat, new smoke was rising—the light gray of burning grass.

A grassfire is nothing like the flamewall. A grassfire is fast and unpredictable, and it burns things without healing them—a true emergency.

"Scarlet, collect the children," my grandmother said, her voice taut like a bowstring. Then she turned to me. "Get to Tycho. And warn him."

Tycho must have heard, I knew. It was a clear day and the whole universe had probably watched the arrival of the not-fish. But I did as she said, my heart racing as I ran to the nearest bicycle.

....

I pedaled as fast as I could to Tycho's wagon, its blue roof a beacon in the distant orchard. I half expected to catch up with him, but he was fast for someone in middle age. Besides, I was using a cargo-bike—geared for towing wagons, not for racing.

When I reached his wagon, I was out of breath. I shouted his name, bursting in through the doors, but Tycho was already gone. Just his stacks of books and gadgets and lenses.

I plunked myself down on the wagon's back step for a few seconds to catch my breath. Where would he have gone in this moment?

Glancing up toward the silver things, it was obvious. Tycho could not have resisted a chance to inspect them more closely. And in the direction of my gaze was a fresh track where the grass had been trampled by Tycho's hasty departure on bicycle.

I followed his trail out of the orchard and then alongside a creek we called Old Man's Leg that ran across the grasslands. The silver not-fish were further than they looked. They must, then, be *bigger* than they seemed.

I neared the smoke without finding Tycho and slowed cautiously as I approached the grassfire, staying close to the creek. I dismounted my bicycle and studied the tracks in the grass. The truth was I had lost the trail. I wasn't sure if these tracks belonged to Tycho alone, or to a Grasslander, or both.

As I knelt to examine the impression of bike tires beside the creek, I thought I heard voices. Not the speech of a Grasslander—which sounded like a breeze through a stand of broomgrass—but someone shouting in a guttural dialect of harsh consonants. Other people. Strangers.

Whoever they were, they were close.

I stood to survey the landscape. The grasslands were mostly flat but shaped here and there by the slow and gentle action of water. The not-fish had landed in a wide, shallow valley. On the east side of the valley was a winding stream. On the west side was an oxbow, a long arc of still water that had been part of the original stream before shifting sediment had moved the whole stream east.

The silver not-fish had all landed in an area largely enclosed by the stream and the oxbow, which I could see had thankfully served to keep the grassfires from spreading too far. But now there was a much graver concern.

The valley was dangerously close to the flamewall, which would sweep through this place sometime in the night. Did these strangers not understand how precarious their position was? It was my job to make sure; we all have to watch out for each other.

"*We keep us safe*," I muttered to myself as I followed the stream on foot toward them.

Servitor Graft

Our descent was bumpy, off-target, and nearly catastrophic. Scitechs at the bottleneck station had injected our drop-pods into a world where physics didn't make sense, where gravity pulled out instead of down, where the land itself loomed both above and below our heads.

Their hasty briefing called it a pocket universe, but there was nothing pocket-sized about it.

« They lied. As usual. »

The Conquis had kept us from crashing to pieces on the inner surface of the massive sphere. When we burst into being—so far from the ground that the air was thinned nearly to nothing—he seized control from the auto-guidance as every alarm blared, managing to set the pods down so gently that only one of them cracked.

« He's an incredible pilot. »

« He's the worst person we've ever met. »

Once our engines shut off, the Conquis burst from the hatch, fire extinguisher in hand, without even bothering to check if the air was clear. While the rest of us were still jamming gas masks over our faces, he was already wading through an orange cloud of nitrogen tetroxide to fight the fire that had flared up on the cracked drop-pod.

We were the first person to secure our mask, the first one out the pod hatch after him. Clouds of smoke from descent engines and burning grass drifted across the landing zone. Through the haze we watched the Conquis empty an entire extinguisher onto the crack in the pod, quenching the blaze and preventing an explosion of fuel that would have turned the pod and everyone in it into a fireball.

As the smoke cleared and the flames dwindled, the Conquis stood for a moment at the base of the drop-pod, gazing up at the sky like a statue of Armored Victory himself. His dented cuirass gleamed in the sunlight, and his green greatcoat flapped majestically in the breeze.

Then he coughed twice, sharply, and beckoned to us.

We rushed to his side, canteen in hand, but our ancestors were unimpressed. « Only a fool would rush into a cloud of toxic gas when he's already missing half a lung. »

He took the canteen and drank deeply, surveying the scene as soldiers emerged from their pods. A moment later, he handed the half-empty canteen back to me. "Graft, get me the chief scientist."

We nodded our assent, but he was already striding away through the ash and smoldering grass. Then we stared up at the continents arcing above and felt like puking.

The strange sense of so much *mass* looming overhead filled us with waves of vertigo. We paused for a moment in the shade of one of the drop-pods and leaned against it. Its armor, a cascade of overlapping ceramic scales the size of dinner plates, clinked softly under our weight. The silvery scales were still warm—just barely—from the fiery descent. They were made to protect the pods from the superheated plasma of orbital reentry or the beam of a gigawatt laser burning a tunnel through the sky. A bit of engine heat and some smoldering grass were nothing to them.

We found the chief scientist disembarking from his drop-pod and brought him to the low ridge where the Conquis stood, hands on hips, glaring up.

"Explain," the Conquis began, jerking his chin at the curve of the land overhead, "what the fuck is going on here."

We knew exactly what he meant. In his service, we had visited many orbital habitats, some wealthy enough to boast vast areas of artificial land under open sky. The biggest were spinning cylinders a few kilometers long, with a handful of ponds they called "lakes" and small parks they called "forests" wedged between sprawling estate grounds.

One of our ancestors had even spent time at a spinning O'Neill Sphere so large that the moisture in its bubble of air condensed and fell as rain, with creeks that drained down to a skinny equatorial trench they called the Sea.

« This is nothing like that. »

Our ancestor was right. The vastness above us was beyond the wealth of any commandant or mining baron. The sphere was so gargantuan that distant mountains faded into blue mist and clouds. But seeing at the opposite side of the sphere was not like viewing a distant mountain; it was like gazing at the surface of a planet from orbit.

This place had not ponds but *oceans.* Where orbital habs had grassy hills concealing air scrubbers, this world had true mountains. It was almost beyond description.

« It's incredible. The most beautiful place since home. »

"Is it spinning?" the Conquis demanded. We could see why he might think so. There was a circular ocean on the near side and a circular desert on the far side, each of which twisted and puckered as though a spin axis might pass from one to the other. Perhaps the bright, lamp-like sun slid along the line between them.

"We'll investigate," the chief scientist replied. "But this is not spin-gravity. There could be an extremely dense substrate beneath the ground."

« Wrong! » insisted an ancestor. « This fool thinks that we are standing inside a sphere of neutronium? » We shook our head to try to clear the insistent voice of memory, but it continued. « Outward gravity is not generated in a hollow shell. Newton himself made these calculations millennia past. Start with a simple recognition that the force of gravity is proportional to the radius squared— »

"If it were a hollow sphere of even thickness," we said, to appease the ancestor, "Sir Isaac Newton showed there would be zero gravity across the entire interior volume." The chief paused, surprised to be addressed so bluntly by a servitor, and then nodded sheepishly.

"Perhaps I should put Graft in charge of the investigation," the Conquis suggested to the scientist.

We felt a momentary stirring of pride until an ancestor put us in our place. « That's a boast, not a compliment. It makes him feel important to have a genius wash his underwear. »

The lieutenant and quartermaster approached. With land and sea looping overhead, they appeared like bats hanging upside-down from the roof of a smoldering cave. We stared at the ground below our feet, doing our best not to vomit.

The Conquis turned to the lieutenant and demanded, "Where the fuck is VANGUARD?"

His second-in-command held a rugged transmitter-receiver, covered in handles and shatter-proof indicators. The beacon's metal housing was bright orange—one of REPO's few uncamouflaged pieces of equipment—so that it could be easily located. Without a beacon, we would truly be lost, so each drop-pod had its own.

"They didn't activate their beacon, sir," his second-in-command replied. "We aren't sure where they made landfall." The lieutenant nodded toward the machine he held. "We haven't received any messages from the bottleneck station, either."

Around us, the other servitors were hastily erecting an improvised command tent. The green canvas they stretched overhead blocked the view of the "sky" and offered some relief from vertigo.

Of course, we *should* have been standing in VANGUARD's tent. The Conquis should have been welcomed with a fanfare of three bugles. VANGUARD should have rained hellfire down on the enemy and then secured a landing zone. But they weren't even answering over radio.

"I want drones in the air," the Conquis said. "I want eyes on the enemy and a defensible perimeter." Servitors were now erecting fabric walls behind him, enclosing the tent.

"Yes, my conqueror," the lieutenant replied, departing at a run.

The Conquis turned to his chief scientist. "You said this was a *pocket* universe. It's fucking huge."

The chief scientist was unrepentant. "We can get more accurate measurements now that we've arrived."

"Then go *measure*," Conquis replied, "and locate the command center, or the power nexus, or whatever we need to capture to control this place."

The chief scientist nodded and shuffled though the doorway, staring at the ground to avoid vertigo.

Only the quartermaster remained.

"Set up camp," the Conquis ordered the man. "Full tent deployment, everything. And once the servitors are done, have them dig a moat. Let's keep any grassfires on the outside."

"Yes, my conqueror," the quartermaster replied.

But as the quartermaster exited the tent, a sentry outside shouted, "Visual contact! Three hundred yards."

The Conquis strode out through the door. We followed, but as we left the tent, we caught another glimpse of the "sky" above. We paused, breathing deeply to suppress the waves of dizziness. A flock of birds passed overhead. We didn't recognize which species. Aside from a few sickly individuals in hab zoos, we'd only ever seen simulated birds in historical dramas.

Downhill, where the creek drained away from camp, the air was hazy, full of smoke and dust. We could hear *something* in that direction—a diffuse cascade of snorts and thumps—but couldn't resolve the source of it through the thick sepia fog.

Autocannons on the nearby drop-pods, which had been panning slowly back and forth like snakes stiffing for prey, snapped over toward the sound, detecting something in infrared that we could not.

We glanced at the Conquis. He pulled back his greatcoat and rested a hand on the butt of his pistol. Nearby soldiers stared into the haze, their weapons pointed in the direction of the sounds. The servitors who had been working around us quietly found shelter behind stacks of half-unloaded equipment. They were not combatants; they had only just been plucked out of the servitor pool for this mission, and were not prepared for such things.

From the source of the sound a shadow appeared—not a human figure but a dark, wide mass. Something coughed, deeply. We could hear footfalls, *dozens* of overlapping footfalls on the dry grass and in the mud of the creek bed.

Then a glimpse of horns and dark fur. Slowly, almost inquisitively, a group of strange animals emerged from the haze, walking so closely together that they were almost a single creature.

« A herd of bison! »

My ancestors recognized these dark-eyed animals, their thick pelts and muscular shoulders. The creatures kept moving, slowly, fearlessly, toward us.

"Conquis?" asked the lieutenant, his open weapon raised toward the creatures.

"Leave it to the autocannons," he replied. For the herd was approaching the formal perimeter, a laser-marked line that the autocannons drew in scintillating red around the edge of the camp.

The animal at the head of the herd stepped through the line, too stupid to understand the meaning of that flickering crimson border. We winced in anticipation, closing our eyes as we waited for the thunder of the autocannons.

Silence. There was silence except for the gentle footfalls of the bison as they approached.

We opened our eyes. At least a dozen bison had crossed fully over the red line, with dozens more behind them. Yet the autocannons had not fired, had not rendered them into burger.

The bison moved with purpose, with curiosity. Perhaps they had never seen a drop-pod or a conquistador.

The Conquis stepped forward to meet them. And while most of the bison paused at his approach, the foremost animal kept walking, like an emissary.

The Conquis and the bison stopped only a few feet from each other. The bison snorted loudly. The Conquis reached out with his left hand toward the bison's broad head, which reached only as high as the bottom of his cuirass. The bison sniffed his fingers curiously. Then the Conquis raised his right arm, pistol in hand, and fired.

The sound sent the herd fleeing even before the lead bison had fully collapsed to the ground. A few soldiers, caught up in the moment, fired spontaneously into the retreating herd before the lieutenant ordered them to stop.

The Conquis beckoned us to approach. We stepped carefully, keeping our eyes on the ground to maintain our balance. Blood was still gushing from the head of the bison, pooling on the grass. The Conquis handed us his pistol so that we could clean it—the antique powder would corrode the barrel if not cleaned promptly.

« This bison is too small », an ancestor told us. On Old Earth, bison had been enormous; easily taller than a human. We had never before seen a bison ourselves on any hab or planet, but this animal had stood much shorter than the Conquis.

The Conquis stepped forward and kicked the animal in its substantial hump. It didn't move. Then he demanded to no one in particular, "What the fuck is this?"

....

The Conquis summoned his command staff. As we walked from the dead bison back to the command tent, we passed stacks of equipment and supplies that servitors were in the process of unloading. They emptied out the cargo compartments and garages at the bottom of each drop-pod, unfolding the battery-powered cargo jeeps inside. The camp was taking shape. On the outside was the rough circle of drop-pods. At the center was a large open rectangle, like a scorched sports field, lined by a perimeter of tents, which was anchored at one end by the large kitchen tent and at the opposite end by the command tent.

Each tent bore, in white, the emblem of the People: a male figure drawn within a circle and square, four arms and four legs showing the ideal human proportions.

« Da Vinci: The Vitruvian Man. »

Generators were already rumbling away, providing electricity for an array of telescoping light standards that would be useful once the sun set—assuming it set.

The camp was like a tiny anthill, each caste carrying out their duties with unquestioning instinct. The other servitors, clad in maroon tunics like ourself, did the heavy lifting. The Scitechs in their white coats deployed expensive sensors and equipment. And the soldiers in green camouflage kept an eye out, scanning the landscape for things to kill.

Accompanying the command staff, we crossed through the middle of the open rectangle toward the command tent and passed a group of Scitechs trying to launch a drone. They couldn't seem to get the drone to rise more than two meters off the ground before it began to wobble and then drop noisily to the burned grass below.

Inside, the other servitors had been busy. By the front doorway was a galley box full of snacks, drinks, and self-heating coffee cans while the tent's interior had been furnished with rugs, tables, chairs, and a few cots in the corners. The orange beacon from the Conquis's drop-pod sat on a table next to a bowl of whole walnuts. The beacon was dark and silent, the two keyholes beside its dial staring sightlessly like dead eyes.

Once we were all inside, the Conquis turned to his lieutenant. "Care to explain why I had to shoot that beast myself," the Conquis asked sourly, "when the autocannons should have turned it into pink mist?"

"Some supplies are missing, my conqueror," said the lieutenant. "Each drop-pod should contain forty thousand rounds of ammunition for the autocannons, all depleted uranium. I checked them myself, before the injection."

The chief scientist, the lieutenant, the quartermaster—they all had *names*, of course, not just ranks. But names implied *humanity*, implied that they might sometimes act out of warmth or generosity.

That expectation would be a mistake.

"And how many rounds do we have?" the Conquis asked sharply.

"I've checked every capsule in REPO force, my conquis," the lieutenant stuttered. "Every drop-pod. This has never happened before, I don't understand how it's even possible, that I, that we—"

"Untie your tongue and tell me, soldier."

"We have no depleted uranium rounds whatsoever," the lieutenant said, blanching. "We have lead-based munitions for the small arms. But none of the DU made it through the injection."

There was a long uncomfortable silence.

« Keep us safe. Don't make the Conquis angry. »

"If VANGUARD had the same problem, that might explain why they crashed," the chief scientist speculated. "Their assault craft would have been too light; the autopilots might have overcompensated. The landing engines can only throttle so low, my conquis, and—"

The Conquis cut him off with a gesture. "So, the autocannons didn't fire because the magazines are empty."

The lieutenant seemed more nervous than we had ever seen him. "There is *also* a problem with the smart systems built into the machines," he explained. "They are malfunctioning, sir. Badly. The drones are having the same issue."

"The squatters have already been here a week," said the Conquis. "Now you're giving them an even bigger head start."

"We lacked time to prepare," the quartermaster protested. "And we're used to dropping onto planets, not into other universes."

The Conquis waved this away. "When will the systems be fixed?"

The lieutenant, the quartermaster, and chief scientist exchanged glances in a silent game of chicken to determine who would take the risk of responding.

"It's not so simple, my conquis," began the quartermaster. "We tried to reboot the fire control system five times. The databanks are . . . corrupted. The autocannons will follow moving objects, but they won't fire."

The Conquis offered a powerful frown, "Is it a hardware problem or a software problem?"

"My conqueror," the chief scientist added, regretfully, "at the nanoscopic level, that is a distinction without a difference. The memory of each smart system is woven from carbon filaments and captured ions, so if the hardware is scrambled, the software is erased, and vice versa. There should be software backups, of course, on other drives—"

This was beyond both the knowledge and the interest of the Conquis, who interrupted sharply. "This is a *combat unit*, gentlemen. If things are damaged, fix them. Why are you complaining to me instead of restoring the software from backups?"

"We would like to," the lieutenant answered, pausing to clear his throat at length. The lieutenant took a long drink of water from his canteen and swallowed, while the Conquis watched him, waiting with a gaze that verged on menace.

"It's just," the lieutenant resumed, "that none of us can quite remember *how*."

....

After the command staff had been angrily dismissed by the Conquis, we waited a long, quiet moment as he huffed to himself.

The Conquis was a practical man, incurious by choice. Another kind of leader might have asked what my ancestors were now asking:

« How could so many tons of ammunition just *disappear*? »

« Was the quartermaster lying? Is this a trick? »

« Did someone sabotage the smart systems? »

« Are the physics of this world more different than we thought? »

But that kind of leader might have stumbled into other existential questions—like questions of morality that could only distract from the mission and impair the combat effectiveness of a Conquistador First Class.

"Bring me amphor," he said, still staring out the doorway.

The hard-sided amphor case sat on a table next to a bowl of unshelled walnuts and the beacon from the Conquis's drop-pod. The case had been gifted to the Conquis by his commandant and was embossed in gold with the words: *Man is the model of the world.*

« We'd best not think about what that means. »

We opened the case. The full bottle of amphor lay comfortably in its felt-lined compartment alongside four small glasses in distinct little alcoves.

Each glass was etched with a different Icon of Triumph. We chose the Icon of Winged Death, auspicious and suitable to a successful landing.

« Did he drink from this glass the day he trampled our gardens beneath his boots? »

We pulled the stopper from the bottle—a sour pungency filled our nostrils—and poured a few fingers of whirling orange liquid into the glass.

Then we paused. There had been a tiny crack in the glass's thick base, just below the talons on Winged Death's left foot. The crack had been there for years, ever since a hard combat landing in the Lush Realm. It was there when we had last polished the glasses.

We turned the glass slowly in the light, trying to find the crack. It was gone. The glass was, once again, as perfect as the day it had been made. Our surprise quieted even the ancestors for a moment.

We brought the Conquis the full glass of amphor. He drained it in a single draw and passed it back to us without acknowledgment. The amphor took effect swiftly, his skin already flushing and his pupils dilating visibly.

Amphor is a powerful stimulant. It wasn't meant for ingestion, really—most people applied it externally to treat inflammation and congestion. But for the Conquis, external use no longer sufficed.

The Conquis breathed in deeply, like a newborn inhaling for the first time, and then strode from the tent with purpose.

We cleaned the glass hurriedly and put it away. But as we did, an ancestor raised another question.

« What if this world can defend itself? »

....

We had a moment of blessed quiet after the Conquis left the tent. We put a hand on the chest of our maroon tunic, where we kept the Souven secreted away. A few hours of rest—a few hours with the Souven—would have been enough to reorient us. To give us precious insights into this strange world or at the very least the memories to know its plants and animals.

« Keep us safe. Survival is all that matters. »

But recuperation wasn't possible, no matter how much we needed it. The Conquis called us only moments later. "Graft, come!"

We hurried out the door, following the Conquis's gaze. Two camp sentries approached, their gray-and-green uniforms offering poor camouflage against the yellow grass of the hills beyond.

Between them was a girl or perhaps a young woman, though she was short enough that she seemed like a child next to the soldiers. Instead of the synthetic, machine-spun clothing we expected of the squatters, she wore a loose textile that appeared almost homemade. She had on her belt what we first presumed to be a knife but on closer inspection found to be a little, rounded shovel, like a trowel.

She was smiling warmly, as if to broadcast an attitude of friendliness and hospitality.

« She's nervous. »

"Well done," the Conquis was saying. "Where did you capture her?"

"Actually, sir," the sentry on the right answered, "she walked right into the camp."

The Conquis frowned at her thoughtfully.

"Hello!" she said. "I'm Char of the Ami, and I am called 'She Who Remembers What Was Given.'"

Her dialect was strange and her accent strong. We barely understood her at first, though on a moment's reflection her speech resembled the technical creole of H-17, a neighborhood frequented by some of my ancestors before our home was ruined.

The Conquis stared at her. Likely he didn't understand half of the words she had said. As usual, when comprehension failed, he fell back on authority.

"You are a wrongful squatter in this world," he informed the girl. "And we are here to repossess it for the People."

Chapter 3

Contact

Char of the Ami

The valley where the strangers had landed formed a kind of natural enclosure. The visitors had stationed glowering men above the valley walls, looming in the tall, dry grass that remained. Stone-faced, they escorted me into their camp and walked me right past a dead and bloody bison.

I could barely understand what the strangers were saying. The loud one with the metal vest was staring at me, talking at me, but his accent was so odd that I couldn't follow his words. Just because we stood in the same place didn't mean we could communicate.

For a moment, I thought he had accused me of squatting, so I stood even straighter. I wanted to make the best possible first impression on behalf of the Ami.

I tried a different dialect, again smiling widely. "Fair grazing," I greeted in the soft tongue of the Grasslanders. "I am Char, proud

Ami gatherer." My pronunciation was impeccable, each consonant like a raindrop on a leaf of clover.

"Speak up, child!" he demanded, though I was not at all a child.

Oh well, being in the grasslands didn't make you a Grasslander. Their strange silver craft reminded me of boats—I could see people climbing in and out of them—so I tried Ternspeech.

"Generous wind!" I whistled, "I am Ami-Char!" I punctuated the greeting with three clicks of respect, but the loud man just stared at me, dark eyebrows furrowed, as though I were a strange bird.

For the first time, I felt my smile falter. I was running out of dialects to try.

A slender man, dressed in baggy clothes the color of clotted blood, appeared at the loud man's elbow and whispered something in his ear.

The loud man nodded, "Yes, Graft." The man called Graft was tall but stooped, his head and shoulders bowed. Graft's hair was shaved on the sides but the hair on top was plastered flat against his scalp, as though with wax.

The tall man faced me, his gentle face unsmiling, and said, "Hello welcome greetings," in serviceable ceremonial speech.

It was a strange thing to hear outside of a Convergence, and the tall man had the accent of a desert preacher. But it gave me something to work with. I clasped my hands in deference to the ceremonial tongue and introduced myself a fourth time. "I am Char, of Ami choir." My pronunciation was rusty, but the tall man nodded and said something to the loud man in their own dialect.

The loud man puffed out his chest and finally introduced himself, "I am Sergeant-Conquistador First Class Mandrel Hannover,

Right Hand of the Commandant, Ravager of Enceladus, and Keeper of the Seventh Gate." He went on in that vein for some time, listing—locations? family members? titles? I understood only parts of what he said, and I wasn't sure if the gap was one of accent or vocabulary.

As he rambled, I noted his uncomfortable clothing—heavy boots, an enormous green coat with a hem that almost dragged on the ground, and beneath that, a dented metal vest embossed with a figure that had four arms and four legs. The man stood on what *had* been a small stand of lowbush blueberries, their ripe fruit needlessly trampled beneath his boots.

"May our voices rise in harmony," I greeted, still unsure if his actual name was Mandrel or Enceladus or something else. "How can I show the hospitality of the Ami?"

"Simple," he answered, in his odd accent. "You can bring me Quang Duc."

Servitor Graft

We watched as the youngster helpfully answered the Conquis's questions. « Don't talk to cops! » an old memory insisted, but it was no use.

Everything about her—her guileless eyes, her open body language, the expressions that flickered unguardedly across her face—*everything* told us the girl had spent a lifetime surrounded by people she could trust and respect.

She could not have been more unprepared to confront the Conquis.

« Help her! » came another flicker. « Warn her. » It was upsetting to watch. Part of us wanted to intervene in that moment. But we felt frozen.

Another thought rationalized our inaction. « It is not kind to warn the lamb of the abattoir. »

« No, these are mainline humans. It's not going to be like last time. »

But even as we watched, something changed. For the first time, the smile dropped from her face. We watched as the girl stuttered. "Quang Duc? Why do you want Quang Duc?"

"He will answer for his crimes," the Conquis declared.

"How could he have committed . . ." The girl seemed flabbergasted. "How do you even know his name?"

"We know everything," the Conquis answered. "We know the names of all the leaders. Quang Duc is the algorithmic expert, but Mandela and Boudica have the most to answer for."

"Mandela and Boudica!" the girl said, surprised anew. "They don't even live among the Ami."

"We will track them down wherever they hide," the Conquis answered. "And Zapata and Tycho."

"Tycho!" the girl seized on the name. "That's my uncle. His wagon is nearby."

"Where? What does it look like?"

« Say nothing! »

She pointed in the direction of a cluster of trees on the curving slope of land beyond, now relieved to be able help. "It has a blue roof and mahogany wheels. Tycho can explain any misunderstandings. He knows a lot."

"I'm sure he does," Conquis growled in reply, nodding to his nearby lieutenant. "In any case, cooperation will serve you well."

"We always cooperate!" the girl answered, more brightly. "It's the Ami way!"

The Conquis nodded. "Very well, Amy," he replied, glad to have gained the upper hand. "In that case, I have more questions." He gestured to us, and we brought forward folding chairs. The two of them sat opposite one another, the Conquis looming over the girl.

She was indeed older than the Conquis had assumed, we could see now. Though much shorter than most adults, she didn't have the face of a child. And her clothes were fit loosely, not the feminine clothing that the People were accustomed to; nor did she wear make-up.

"Now then," he asked, "where is your headquarters?" Her face took on a quizzical expression; perhaps the accent was still interfering. "The command center? The bunker? Where do Tycho and the other leaders give their orders?"

"Tycho doesn't give orders," she said. "He just teaches. Everyone makes up their own minds about what to do."

« The Iter are non-hierarchal. They prize autonomy and self-determination. »

"No doubt," answered the Conquis, an eye roll barely suppressed. "But where is the central command post? The control panel for this universe?"

The young woman again seemed confused. "I don't know what that is," she said. "Each people walk their own path."

The Conquis narrowed his eyes, trying to decide whether she was lying or merely an ignorant child. "When you came through the injector," he said, "where did you put your equipment? Your supplies?"

"What's an injector?" she asked.

He scoffed. "The *machine*," he said, growing frustrated. "The machine that takes objects and people from the prime cosmos and pushes them into this pocket universe." Her face was blank. "The *big box* covered in *metal coils* that you went through to get to this place."

She pursed her lips toward one side, then answered. "I was born here in Germinal."

"That's ridiculous," he answered. "It's been a week. How stupid do you think I am?"

"I don't think you are very stupid at all!" she answered, encouragingly.

"What is your station?" he demanded, in a growl. "And how old are you?"

"I study mechanics and medicine. And I'm eighty-nine laps," she replied. Then clarified, "Twenty-two years."

We heard a muffled gasp from behind us. The chief scientist had approached to watch the interrogation and seemed genuinely shocked by her statement.

The hairs on the back of our neck begin to rise.

Even the Conquis was taken aback, "You are twenty-two years old? How could you have been born here?"

"Through the flamewall," she answered. "Same as everybody."

« You must stop this. »

"My conqueror!" we said. Even as he shot us a sharp look for interrupting, we continued, "A sentry approaches!"

Char of the Ami

I did not understand how Conquis could know so little. Perhaps the dialect barrier was part of the problem, but any eight-year-old in Germinal knew more about how the world worked. Such ignorance would put all these people in danger, especially so close to the flamewall. I suspected the tall, skinny man—Graft—understood most of what I was saying, but he just stared at the ground whenever I tried to catch his eye.

I was about to suggest that I could invite someone from Tapestry (dialogue was their specialty, after all) when yet another man—a hunter?—approached. The young man held a Grasslander bow, which he handed to Conquis. They exchanged a few whispered words as Conquis inspected the bow.

Then Conquis turned back to me. "This bow. This is not a bent sapling with a piece of leather string," he said. "It's a compound crossbow. A sophisticated machine." He gestured at my clothing. "Do you think you can fool me with this homespun get-up and rawhide sandals?"

"How did you get this bow?" I asked. I wondered if he had dug it up.

He ignored me. "Where are your *factories*?"

"Factories?" I asked, uncertain.

"You can't hunt this polymer cable," he said, gesturing again. "You can't cast aluminum pulleys over a campfire. Where do you *manufacture* things?"

This was a word I knew, at least in part, and I brightened with recognition. "Oh, we don't make them by *hand*," I explained. "They're too complicated for that. We make them underground."

"Obviously," he said, glaring. "Where is the entrance to the factory? The control bunker? The service hatches?"

This made little sense, but I did my best to answer. "You can dig anywhere," I said. "As long as you remember where you buried it."

I could see from the way the scars on his chin curled in on themselves that my response displeased him greatly.

"We found this half-buried in a container beneath a landing engine," he said. "How many of these weapons caches do you have?"

"Yes, caches!" I tried helpfully. "Do you have something that needs to be fixed? The flamewall is almost here. You can bury it right now before you move camp."

"We're not going anywhere," he answered.

The whole conversation had been a spiral of growing confusion, but this answer baffled me most of all. Late autumn was a time to *move* camp not set up a new village. But I could see around me that the men—they were all men, as far as I could guess—were digging trenches and putting up tents and driving poles into the ground. It was strange and unnerving; like watching a bird build a nest in a tree that had already turned the orange of autumn. Was it possible they didn't realize the flamewall was so close?

I explained it then as I would to a child. "The flamewall will be here in a few hours. If you don't move, it will burn up all of your things." And the people, of course, but that went without saying.

"We're not afraid of a grassfire," he answered. "I've burned down whole planets." My eyes widened. "We've cleared a perimeter around the camp," he said. "Dug trenches to extend the stream into a moat. Dammed the creek to make a firefighting reservoir. There will be some smoke, but any fires will flow right around us."

For the first time, I realized that something was deeply wrong.

"Water won't stop the flamewall," I said, standing to emphasize my point. From behind me, a firm hand clamped onto my shoulder. I turned to see a man dressed in gray and green, like a hunter. "Let go of me," I said. To my surprise, he did not react. These strangers lacked knowledge even of basic etiquette.

When I reached up to remove his hand myself, the leader barked, "Enough!" The hunter released me and stepped back.

I half-turned back to Conquis, keeping the hunter in the corner of my eye. "The flamewall can burn through anything. Unless you are finished living this life, you will move before it arrives."

He stepped very close to me so that even with both of us standing he could stare straight down at me. "That's the last time you ever threaten me. Chief, take your measurements." And then he walked off into his gigantic green tent.

Servitor Graft

The chief scientist approached, measuring tape in hand. The end of the tape wriggled slightly, as if alive. "Stand," he told the girl without making eye contact. "Arms up." She obeyed, confused.

He began to take measurements of her body—height, length of arms, circumference of head, distance from ear to ear—as the tape shifted helpfully to conform to each body part.

« Disgusting. The science of phrenology was long dead even in my time. »

« It was never a science in the first place. »

As the chief scientist measured, he asked a series of questions. "You are twenty-two years old?" he demanded, writing down the length of each individual finger. She nodded.

"How long is a year?"

"A year is four laps of the world," Char answered, as if it were obvious.

"How long can you hold your breath underwater?" he asked, measuring the distance between her eyes as she flinched.

"I don't know. A minute or two."

"Do you know which amino acids you can synthesize, and which are essential?"

"What does that mean?"

He ignored this and measured the circumference of her waist though she leaned away. "Gestation period?" he asked. When she didn't answer, he clarified with irritation, "The *length* of *time* the *fetus* spends in the *uterus*?" emphasizing almost every word.

He seemed to think she was stupid and that he could overcome this by speaking more loudly.

« Step in now! »

There was a galley box by the door of the tent. We pulled two canisters of coffee from the galley box, twisted their bottoms to heat them, and walked toward the pair.

« It's dangerous—don't interfere. »

« Yes, do it! »

We offered one of the canisters to the chief, who refused it with a glare of annoyance and mild contempt. We held the other out to the girl. She glanced at it in bewilderment, then at us.

When we made eye contact, she seemed startled? We don't know what she saw—« Fear! »—but after that her face became less animated, more wary.

She took the can of coffee, her eyes flicking back and forth between our face and the chief's. We backed away, head bowed, watching through our eyebrows from a safe distance.

They kept talking back and forth, the chief's questions becoming more insistent. He tried a different tack, encouraged her to enjoy the coffee. She took one sip and her face wrinkled at the bitterness.

« Bitter is the taste of poison! »

The chief got louder, visibly angry then, and the girl clamped her mouth shut and glared. He stood and the guards who had hung back stepped forward. "Keep her here," the chief instructed.

We followed the chief into the command tent. "She's short but within two standard deviations of the norm," he reported.

The Conquis had been comparing notes with his lieutenant and answered without glancing up. "Not surprising. It's only been a week," he said. "How much could they have diverged?"

The chief frowned. "Something else may be going on," he said. "Our measurements of the physical constants of this universe—"

"Can be conducted without constantly interrupting me," the Conquis said sharply. "Stop acting like a nervous schoolgirl. We've taken back dozens of worlds for the People. This is no different."

« It's incredibly different. »

We knew it, our ancestors knew it, and the chief knew it. But rather than confronting the Conquis, the chief said simply, "More research is required."

"Then do it," the Conquis replied. "And when you can explain where to find VANGUARD and my missing uranium, you'll have my full attention."

Char of the Ami

After Graft and Chief went into the tent, I sat on the chair, stunned. With my grandmother I had attended many meetings between nations, several Convergences, and even tense conciliations between experimental desert polities. Never had I seen anyone touch a stranger without permission or invitation and certainly not as rudely as the hunter and Chief had touched me. My skin crawled at the thought of it.

It began to dawn on me that I had made a series of very wrong assumptions. I had done everything I could to welcome these people and make a good impression, to offer Ami hospitality and win their respect. I had followed all the lessons my parents had taught me.

But nothing these people did or said made any sense. They were rude—not in the prickly way of a desert polity or of a person who wanted to be left alone but in a way that verged on contempt. They were aggressive—not in the boisterous style of the Grasslanders after a hunt but in a way I couldn't then articulate. They were ignorant—not in the way of a child who is learning something for the first time but in the way of someone who didn't even *want* to learn in the first place.

They were willfully stupid, and that put *everyone* in danger.

It was time to leave. I was in over my head. I needed to talk to my grandmother or to someone from Tapestry or to Tycho.

Tycho. I had told these people exactly where he lived. Where to find him. I began to fear that I had made an enormous mistake.

Shaking off a paralyzing sense of dread, I stood and turned toward the edge of the camp, the way from which I had come. The body of the dead buffalo was still there, its blood dried, a cloud of flies circling above its head.

I took two steps before one of the hunters intercepted me. "Sit," he said. I took a step to the left; he moved to block me. "Sit," he repeated more loudly.

"I'm leaving," I told him. I don't know if he even understood, but his companion picked up one of the folding chairs and pushed it behind me so that it struck the back of my knees. Caught off balance, I fell back into it. I flushed with anger and surprise.

The hunter in front of me seemed satisfied. "Sit," he nodded, confiscating the trowel from my belt as if it were dangerous.

I looked up at the land beyond the ridges around us. I could see a dark herd of bison a few kilometers away, but no human figures were in sight.

Then, perhaps five kilometers to the east, where grassland met thick forest, I saw a glint of something at the edge of the canopy. Light reflecting off a lens. I resisted the urge to wave or call out. Hopefully the sight of me with two hostile hunters would be enough to broadcast my distress.

Conquis, his metal vest clanking, emerged from the big tent. "We will have more questions for you," he told me. "Graft is going to make you comfortable in the meantime."

"I am ready to—" I began.

"Graft," Conquis interrupted me firmly, almost angrily, "is going to make you comfortable." He pointed to a smaller tent nearby.

In that moment I could have tried to run. But my mind told me I didn't need to run, not to worry, that it was just a misunderstanding. And my gut told me not to do anything that would make the huge man angry.

Servitor Graft

The irony of making someone "comfortable" in a prison was not lost on me. The tent where the squatter was to be detained didn't *look* like a prison. It looked like a drab, claustrophobic storage tent with space for a few cots, the ceiling so low that the top of our head brushed the canvas roof. So, for the time being, all of us—the girl, the Conquis, ourself—would pretend it was merely a tent.

"May we bring you something to eat?" we asked.

Char ignored the offer. "Where are you from?" she asked us.

We paused because there were so many answers. « A village of bright fabric. »

« A moon covered in ice as smooth as glass. »

« An ocean that spanned a whole world. »

We paused so long that she continued. "I mean, is it a home like ours?"

"We grew up on an Isola–Verdant Type III habitat, orbiting a white dwarf," we answered honestly. The confusion in her eyes was evident, so we added, "A kind of village built into a comet. It was a bit like this place, with floors and rooms that curved up to the sky. But it wasn't a sphere. It was made of wheels; there wasn't enough space for trees or bison."

She brightened at the implication of common ground. "So, we're from the same type of place!" she said. "We're not enemies at all!"

We kept our face neutral. Enemy or not, our role was unchanged.

"Why did you leave your home?" she asked.

A clamor in our mind. « Empire. »

« Evil men! »

« Inevitable catastrophe. »

« We were conscripted to invade this place. To do to you what was done to us. »

Instead, we gave a technically precise and meaningless answer. "After the stellar harvesting, our star became an unstable red dwarf. We had to leave."

« Starlifters squeeze stellar fragments from a white dwarf. Comet melts as fragile habitat breaks into shards. »

"Oh!" she said, not fully understanding. "I'm sorry that happened to you and to Conquis and your friends."

« The Conquis *did* it! »

« They are not our friends. »

"*We* had to leave," we said, tapping our own chest. "The Conquis and the others are from . . . a different place."

"*You* had to leave?" Char asked, confused.

"We did. But we carry with us memories from those who did not survive. And so, to honor and recognize them—"

"You use the word 'we,'" she said, nodding. Clearly, she wasn't as naive as she had first seemed.

« She can understand. You should help her. »

« The Conquis expects you to get information. You've got to bring him something. »

"The Conquis will offer mercy," we said. "If you tell him the truth."

"I told the truth," Char replied.

"He wants to know why your people stole the nature preserve," we said. "The park, that the Iter were—" « Conscripted. Kidnapped. » "—hired to build."

"Nature preserve?" she said, furrowing her brow.

"This microcosm," we waved vaguely upward. "It was supposed to be a nature preserve for the People." « The elite, the rich. »

"But once it was finished, instead of handing it over, your people rebelled and fled into it. Tycho himself set the bomb that damaged the injector so you couldn't be followed."

"Tycho didn't do that," she insisted.

We thought of the memory loss that the Scitechs had experienced, unable to recall how to troubleshoot basic equipment. Could something about this place *erase* unwanted memories? To offer the squatters a clean slate? To rid them of trauma?

« Trauma they had plenty of. »

« To forget is a luxury of the privileged. To remember is our duty. »

"Why did you warn us?" she asked. "When the chief was talking to us about babies?"

"We didn't!" we insisted, our voice hushed.

« Just admit it. Tell her the truth. »

"The People—the Conquis and his culture—they have very *specific* ideas about what it means to be human," we explained.

« They are human supremacists! »

"Many groups in the human diaspora have . . . adapted to local conditions in ways that the People disagree with. They have altered their bodies and their genes to thrive in places that would kill mainline humans."

"What is human diaspora?" Char asked.

"We are!" we exclaimed. "All of us. You, your people, ourself, the Conquis, the soldiers, the Scitechs, the pilots, the other servitors. All of us came from Earth, in the beginning."

"Oh, from the inside-out universe!" she realized.

"Yes!" we answered.

« It must be nice to forget so much. »

"It was a harsh place," she said, "which made for harsh people."

"It still exists," we declared. "And there is . . . was a lot of variety."

« Mer-people living on water worlds covered in thick islands and continents of algae. Thick-furred humans hibernating in tunnels on ice planets above gas giants. Long-limbed spider-humans in asteroid mines orbiting singularities. Heavy desert worlds where humans live in flooded lagoons to keep double gravity from crushing them. Humans adapted, genetically transformed to fit every world they found. »

« And the Conquis spent a lifetime wiping them out. »

"He's on a crusade," we finished.

"So, you think the Conquis will feel threatened by our babies?"

« Don't speak of it! Don't ask. It's better not to know. »

"Whatever you do," we said. "Do *not* talk to the Conquis about babies."

We needed to leave. We had been in the tent for several minutes and the Conquis might grow suspicious. But the topic had reminded her of something else.

"The flamewall!" she said. "It's close."

"A grassfire won't frighten the Conquis," we said, moving to leave. "We'll talk later."

As we went to go, she followed us out of the tent. "Stay in the tent," we warned. But it was too late. The Conquis was coming out of the command tent with fire in his eyes.

Char of the Ami

The Conquis marched up to me, with two hunters behind him. He exchanged rapid words with Graft, too quickly for me to follow. Then he turned and glared down at me. "I told you to stay in the tent."

"Every person has the freedom to leave," I replied. This fact was fundamental. And yet Conquis frowned to hear me say it. Behind him, Graft eyed the ground.

"And the chief tells me you stopped answering his questions."

"I will choose when I speak and when I don't," I replied. Another fundamental right.

Conquis sighed. "So be it."

He went over to a stack of boxes on a cargo pallet. Men in maroon had been working there but scattered silently as Conquis approached. He pulled out a large plastic strap with ridges like scales on one side and a bulge like a head with a mouth at one end. It twitched slightly in his fingers.

Then he stepped back toward me and seized my left arm. Before I could pull away, he snapped it over my upper arm between my bicep and my deltoid. With a hiss, it cinched snugly into place, a snake eating its own tail.

Conquis let go, and I stared at it, horrified. Three lights on it winked slowly, like eyes.

"Do you know what that is?" he asked. I shook my head and reached for the loop around my arm. "Don't touch it. It knows where you are. If you try to leave the camp it will sense that. And it will constrict, tighter and tighter, until it cuts your arm off."

I froze, my fingers a few centimeters from the plastic loop, disbelieving his words.

"The same thing will happen if you try to remove it. If you tamper with it in any way, it will slice your arm off your body. You'll bleed to death."

Reflexively, I looked to the people nearby for their help, for intervention. Graft stared at the ground. One of the guards watched me with a snarl, the other with a smirk.

I raised my eyes to the edge of the forest, where I had seen the glint of light earlier. The Conquis followed my gaze. I don't know if he saw something or not, but he acted swiftly.

"Put her back inside the tent," he said. "We don't want her exchanging any messages with her co-conspirators."

One of the guards grabbed my right arm and hauled me back to the small tent, shoving me inside. Through the door I caught a glimpse of the flamewall, only hours away, before the door flap was pulled shut.

Servitor Graft

The Conquis and ourself returned to the command tent. He gestured silently for amphor. We retrieved the amphor case from where it sat next to the beacon and poured him a glass.

The ancestors were not impressed by his theatrics. « Cruel and unnecessary. » The ratcheting device he had clamped onto the girl's arm was used to electronically label shipments for cargo drones in loading bays. Without those cargo drones, it was a glorified zip tie.

As the Conquis sipped his drink, we asked, "Why the elaborate story? Why not just handcuff the girl to something heavy?"

He swallowed a mouthful of amphor and sighed. "It's something the Commandant taught me," he explained. "If I had handcuffed her to a cargo pallet, she'd have spent the next few hours thinking about how to escape. She would try to pick the lock or cut through the plastic or hide a sharp rock in her pocket so she could hit a guard and run away." He took another sip and swallowed. The light coming from outside was turning the red of sunset.

"Not now. She's there thinking, how sensitive is this thing? Could it go off by accident? She's imagining the boundaries of the camp and giving them a wide berth. She's thinking, how can I be friendly and helpful so they'll take this off before it kills me?"

He tipped the glass back and finished the amphor. "We have shifted the burden of ensuring compliance from us onto her. We don't have to police her. She is learning to police herself."

« Interesting theory. Didn't work so well with the Iter. »

The Conquis passed the glass back to me and crossed to the open door of the tent. In front of us, the sun was sinking slowly into the circular ocean at the pole of the world, sliding into a whirling vortex of waves a dozen kilometers across. We could hear a distant, uneven rumble, like a ship's engine throttling down.

Beneath the sound, the Conquis muttered to himself. "The purpose of man is to shape nature," he said softly, as if repeating a mantra. "When nature shapes man, he ceases to be human."

Then, in a commanding shout, he called out the opening of the tent to his lieutenant, "You have the watch!"

The Conquis closed the door flap and hung his greatcoat on a portable coat rack. He gestured for me to help remove his dented cuirass, which latched at one side under the armpit and hinged open on the other side. We carefully slid it off his body. The skin underneath was pale and waxy, except for red welts on the shoulders and hips where they bore the weight of the armor. Around his neck was tied a simple piece of cord holding a multi-pronged silver key that sat above his bare sternum.

"It's time for rest," he said. "Why don't you spend a few hours with your dream machine?"

....

Before lying down, we ducked out of the tent for a moment to see if our vertigo would be diminished by the dark. We spent a moment gazing up at the strange sky above. Here and there in the grasslands that arced over our head, we could see specks of light like distant bonfires. Long, thin lines—grassfires?—were visible as a glow beneath their shroud of smoke. There were moving lights, too, like the pulsing fireflies of a station arboretum, drifting slowly across the sky at some great distance. Flat, rocky mesas of different hues reflected some of the ambient light.

There may have been organic sounds from the grassland nearby, some restless birds or howling predators, but we couldn't hear anything over the camp's rumbling generators.

We went back inside. The Conquis was studying at a tactical map and wouldn't sleep tonight—the amphor ensured it—but he wouldn't need us for a few hours.

We set up our cot in a corner of the command tent and reached for the pouch inside our tunic. We had only two personal possessions. The Souven, of course, irreplaceable and as much a part of our identity as it was a physical object. And a single acorn, embalmed in transparent resin, that had been passed down for generations in the stale hope that it might one day be replanted.

We drew the Souven from its pouch. « Finally! » It was fashioned of something like soft leather and shaped to match our own skull.

« Like an old-fashion aviator's helmet! », recollected one ancient ancestor.

We pulled it onto our head where it fit snugly against our scalp—powerful magnets positioned against the shaved skin on the sides of our head to activate the temporal lobes of our brain. A well-worn strap of vat-leather under the chin kept it in place.

We settled the goggles over our eyes, which illuminated gently and immediately. The Souven had no on switch; it knew when we were there, knew our moods, our thoughts, our struggles.

It contained the entirety of our remaining cultural heritage. Whatever memories hadn't been snuffed out by the Conquis, the Commandant, and the rest of the People.

« Welcome back, child! », came a voice we heard from within our own mind.

At first, the goggles displayed a gentle pattern of ocean waves, accompanied by the hush of water lapping on a beach.

« You've had such a long day », came an ancestor's soft and sympathetic voice. « Here are some memories to help you rest. »

The sound of wind through trees came through the speakers, and in the goggles, we saw palm fronds in moonlight. We breathed in and out deeply, our sighs like a sea breeze through mangroves.

« Just rest », the ancestors encouraged. « You don't need to work, now. We will remember for you. »

We closed our eyes. Yet the images of trees remained; the Souven projected them directly through our neurons, magnetic tendrils coaxing our synapses like gentle fingers plucking a harp. Transferring the memories we might need from the storage of the Souven into our own mind, so we could hear ancestral voices—recall ancestral facts—even after the sacred machine was removed, folded safely into its pouch.

The Souven began to share information on the Iter, « An

anarchistic cultural tradition with offshoots including the Trojan Diggers, the Voleurs, and most infamously, Black Lotus. Political dissidents known for their expertise in subcosmic algorithms. Surviving members were conscripted as a group after their failed escape attempt at 61 Cygni. »

But we needed rest, not another culture's burden. The Souven felt our resistance and switched seamlessly to memories of gentle ecology.

Our body was exhausted, and we slipped easily into the dream memories. Memories of planets, of trees and grass, of flowers and herbs both dangerous and friendly. Of ancestors gardening in the sun and shade. Of a life as an ornithologist. Of a hunt across a wide, verdant valley. We could rest. And remember things we might need when morning came.

....

We awoke when our cot shifted abruptly, and we pulled off our goggles.

"Are you done with your dream machine?" the Conquis demanded. He loomed over us, one boot on the cot. We felt a burst of shame for sleeping in later than he, until we realized that it was still dark out and that the Conquis hadn't slept at all. "Coffee. Breakfast. Battle. In that order."

He had already put on his weathered cuirass, the embossed crest of the Vitruvian Man prominent over his heart.

We tucked the Souven away and rose to make food for the Conquis. But a whistle from a sentry prompted the Conquis to rush out of the tent. We followed.

In the dim light of the foreign and wriggling stars, we could see two figures on the ridge beyond the edge of camp. They stood awkwardly, bow-legged; we realized a moment later that they were straddling a tandem bicycle.

« A bicycle built for two! »

The figure at the rear of the bicycle dismounted and stepped forward.

"I am Tycho!" he called down from the top of the ridge. "I understand you've been looking for me."

Chapter 4

The Flamewall

Char of the Ami

I hadn't been able to sleep in the strange tent and felt exhausted. They had given me a cot, but I was too preoccupied by the snake around my arm to rest, too worried that if I nudged it the wrong way it would explode into violence and sever my arm from my body.

So, when I heard Tycho's voice come over the thrum of the strangers' machinery, I was overjoyed. I burst out of the front flap of the tent, stopping with one foot on the threshold.

"Tycho!" I called back.

He whistled to me in Tern speech, which was meant to be heard over crashing waves and carried easily over the growl of the generators. "Are you hurt?"

"No," I whistled back. "But in danger."

Conquis emerged from his big tent. When he spoke, his voice came from the light stands around as if amplified.

"Tycho," he boomed. "You've made the right decision. Come down with your hands raised."

"Send Char home," Tycho replied, his voice soft and quiet in comparison, "and I will."

"The girl is safe," Conquis replied. "Come down, answer a few questions, and we will let her go."

Part of me wanted to warn Tycho to stay on the ridge, to run away. But another part wished that everything might still be a simple misunderstanding, a cross-cultural mix-up Tycho could fix with his experience and knowledge. Indecision made my voice catch in my throat.

There was a brief, inaudible exchange between Tycho and the Grasslander steering the bicycle. Even in the dark I recognized her as Boudica. By her gestures, she clearly didn't want Tycho to descend. But he came anyway, jogging down the hill toward the camp, directly toward me. He slowed as he approached the perimeter, but he didn't raise his arms. He walked forward with dignity.

The soldiers intercepted him, took his belt trowel, patted him all over as if trying to find something hidden. Then they escorted him the rest of the way into the rectangle at the center of the camp.

Servitor Graft

We watched the man, Tycho, come willingly. It was a strange thing to see. The girl had been young and inexperienced. But here was a leader from the group of insurgents—« Clever freedom-fighters! »—who had stolen an entire universe out from under the nose of the Commandant.

« Perhaps he cares about this girl so much that he would walk willingly into a trap. »

The guards treated him more roughly than they had the girl, shoving him onto the ground at the feet of the Conquis. Even sprawled, it was obvious that he was no taller than Char.

"You have a lot to answer for, traitor Tycho," the Conquis said.

"I will answer your questions," Tycho said, "but send Char home first, as you promised."

"You are the girl's uncle?" the Conquis asked skeptically. "There is no resemblance."

"Kinship transcends appearance."

« The Iter reject traditional family structure in favor of collective childrearing and multi-parent zygotes. They prefer collective ownership over private inheritance. »

"Hmm," the Conquis said, looking the man up and down. "Given what happened on the bottleneck station before you left," the Conquis said, "I had expected more of a fight."

"The path of the Ami is not to fight," Tycho answered, "but to live our lives in peace and freedom."

« The Iter used nonviolent tactics in their opposition to stellar harvesting but joined the diaspora after the re-allocation of Earth's residual biomass. »

"Flowery words," the Conquis said. "But a person who has committed the crimes you have doesn't deserve freedom."

Tycho frowned. "What crimes?"

The Conquis shook his head, disappointed. "Tycho, playing stupid won't work with me. I know exactly who you are and what you've done. I have your criminal record right here." He waved at us, and we hurried to pull the clipboard from his bag.

Leafing through, the Conquis announced each of Tycho's crimes. "Acts of Public Defiance! Sedition. Conspiring with anarchists, socialists, radicals of every stripe. Opposition to property. Research without a license. Et cetera. Sentenced to make restitution to the People via science for the public good." The Conquis shook his head and handed the clipboard back to us. "They gave you a chance to pay your debt to society. To build something worthwhile. A paradise park! And you betrayed them. Was it worth it? To spend a week here before we took it back?"

Tycho was shaking his head, "I don't understand what you're saying, and the flamewall is too close. Let Char go, then we can discuss this in a safer place."

The Conquis sneered. "Enough bullshit, Tycho. Give me the keys to the castle. If you tell Quang Duc and Mandela to surrender, I will ask the Commandant to treat the children with mercy."

We heard Char's sharp inhalation nearby.

Tycho's expression was one of genuine horror. "You would threaten our children?"

"You should have thought about your children before you stole this universe, Tycho. It's not up to me anymore. It's up to the Commandant."

"This is a misunderstanding," Tycho said. "Let's speak to the Commandant."

"He'll arrive soon enough," the Conquis replied. "If you want his mercy, surrender now. Hand over control of this universe to me."

"No one can control Germinal," Tycho said. "Or her people. We are free and we walk our own path."

« *Iter*, from Latin, meaning "the way or the path." Root of the word *iterate*: to repeat or act recursively toward a goal. »

"You've spent the week camping," the Conquis declared. "Enough with these delusions of grandeur."

« Something very strange is going on », an ancestor advised.

We checked the clipboard in our hands. According to his file, Tycho was thirty-three years old. But the man the Conquis was interrogating had gray hair and was easily in his fifties, if not older. We turned our gaze to the starlit microcosm above. The mature forests. The herds of bison.

« This is the work of years, not days. » A chill passed through us. « Once two universes split, why should time pass at the same rate for both? »

What if Tycho looked different because he had been here for decades? What if the girl was telling the truth? What if she genuinely *had* been born here after the Iter refugees arrived and she knew no other world?

The idea was so startling that we lost track of the conversation in front of us, until Char's voice cut in sharply.

"Enough!" she said. "Leave him alone and let us go before the flamewall comes!"

Char of the Ami

I felt a sense of simmering pride at my moment of defiance. Then the Conquis called over his shoulder, "Servitor Graft!" and the tall, thin man stepped forward, eyes toward the ground.

Conquis didn't make eye contact with Graft but instead spoke about him as if he weren't there. "Graft's people used to be proud," he said, "but we taught them humility. Kneel, Graft."

The tall man slumped silently, almost gracefully, to his knees.

The leader circled the man as he spoke. "When we arrived at Graft's home, most of his people were helpful. Cooperative. Good hosts. But when we asked them—very politely—to share their hydroponic decks with us, they hesitated. They questioned us."

I must have appeared confused. "Do you know what hydroponic means?" he asked. I shook my head; Tycho said nothing. Conquis pulled a knife from his belt—I jerked back reflexively—and reached down to the ground, plunging the knife-tip into the soft soil. He dug through the ash with his knife, then rose with a handful of soil in his left hand. He slipped the knife back into the sheath at his hip.

"Hydroponics means to grow food without dirt," he said, observing me coldly. "It's sterile and clean. For Graft here, who grew up in a hab, this handful of dirt might as well be shit." He titled his head slightly toward the kneeling man but kept his eyes on me. "Open your mouth, Graft."

The leader placed his right palm on the man's smooth, waxed hair, tilting Graft's head back to raise the poor man's face toward the sky. Then Conquis poured dirt from his cupped hand into Graft's mouth. Some of the soil spilled onto the kneeling man's nose and upper lip. I watched in shock as Conquis used his fingertips to brush the spilled soil carefully into Graft's mouth, then push his fingers deep into the man's mouth, shoving the soil past his tongue and into the back of his throat. Graft made a soft gagging sound.

Conquis straightened, then wiped his fingers on the kneeling man's loose clothing.

"They gave us their hydroponic gardens," he said, "and then they gave us everything else. They learned not to question. Swallow, Graft."

I watched unbelieving as the kneeling man choked down the

dirt and his glance flitted from face to face to see if anyone might intervene. But the spectators were passive, many dressed in clothes much like the kneeling man's, and they, too, stared at the ground. The hunters, in their green and black, stood watching the man with enjoyment or—even worse—watching *me.*

"Graft thanks me every day for rescuing him from that place," the leader said. "And once we finish with you people, you'll be thanking each one of us, too."

I glanced at Tycho, who looked back, aghast.

The Conquis spoke so quietly that I could barely hear him over the crackling of the flamewall nearing the edge of camp. "Tycho, this is your last chance. Give me what I want."

Tycho glared at him in disgust, then gestured directly toward the approaching flamewall. "If your people stay here," he said, "you will die."

Servitor Graft

The grit scraping between our teeth and prickling in our throat was vile. We wanted nothing more than to run, to go back into the tent and wash out our mouth and lay down with the comfort of the Souven. But we knew something more, something terrible was going to happen.

The Conquis bowed his head—an outsider might have mistaken that as a gesture of pensive humility. But we recognized the silent rage that came before swift violence.

Raising his head, the Conquis pointed to the Ami man and barked, "Box him up!"

The soldiers beside him seized Tycho's arms, cuffing his hands behind his back, their motions swift, practiced, and implacable.

A third soldier wheeled over a wire mesh box—« A cage! »—big enough to fit a large dog. A cluster of long, narrow tanks was bolted to one edge. We could make out a few coils of tubing tucked inside the crate, their ends obscured by wrappings of sterile plastic.

The guard parked the box beside Tycho. Reaching inside, he pulled out a dark shape wrapped in plastic; he peeled away the plastic to reveal a kind of mask with rubber seals—meant to cover the entire face—which was attached via a long, ribbed hose to machinery deep inside the box. With a single efficient motion, the guard slid the mask over the man's face and strapped it firmly against his skull.

The man didn't struggle but stood there with a kind of dignity, breathing through the air hose.

« Courage. »

« Unbending. »

« Futile. »

Then the guard retrieved a second plastic-wrapped module from the box. This one was attached to a narrow, translucent tube that seemed to twitch as it uncoiled. The soldier unwrapped the packaging from its end, and we turned away but not before catching a glimpse of the thing.

« Like a scorpion with a stinging tail, its legs clasp the victim's skin. »

Even in our peripheral vision, we could still see its long, sharp probe in motion. « The stinger seeks its victim's most vulnerable point. » The guard pressed it against the man's collarbone and its razor probe wriggled enthusiastically, pushing easily through papery skin, past bone, and into the chest, finding an artery. The man reacted then, struggling pointlessly to free his hands, to stop the thing burrowing into his body.

Too late. The thing's claws had latched and clamped it into place, and the man slumped forward into the grip of his captors. Blue fluid gushed through the translucent tube between the man and the box, becoming tinged with pink as it reached him.

We felt faint just watching it, a sickening dizziness as the guards folded the old man up and stuffed him roughly into the wire box. We caught a glimpse of Char's watching face, racked with vicarious agony as they dragged her back to her tent. We nearly retched before an ancestor came to our rescue.

« Cold sleep », it said calmly. « An old method of rest for long journeys under heavy acceleration. With help from sedatives, the passenger would sleep deeply in a soft compartment, with intravenous lines to provide nourishment and remove waste. Synthetic gel cushioned the body against high-G, while a respirator assisted the passenger with breathing. A gentle way to travel the stars. »

They closed the lid after the old man, locking it shut, and then one pressed a button that quickly filled the voids in the box with an expanding polymer froth.

« Synthetic gel. »

« Spray foam! » After it had filled every empty space, the compound began to solidify, sealing the man in place. We could see just a bit of skin, perhaps an elbow, where it pressed against the mesh. Only a slow, rhythmic hiss from the breathing machinery told us he was still alive.

« He's cargo now », lamented an ancestor who had once been cargo themself.

A servitor backed a jeep up to the scene; its beeping reverse signal mocked us all with a call for safety. The guards lifted the breathing box easily into the open back of the vehicle.

"Oh," said the Conquis, raising a finger as if the thought had just occurred to him. "Make sure to leave sedation off. Let's give him some time to think about what he's done." There were a few harsh clicking sounds from the breathing apparatus, as if someone were fighting against its valves and pumps, before they drove the box away.

Char of the Ami

They shoved me back into the tent without saying a single word.

"Let him go!" I screamed through the open tent door. "We should *all* leave! The flamewall is here!" But no one answered. I kicked the cot over, my heart pounding with rage over what they had done to my uncle.

And fear at the approach of the flames.

On the grand scale, the flamewall moved with clockwork consistency. But at the human scale, it was idiosyncratic—it would rush down a hill or over a rocky plain but lag behind on a waterway or creep slowly up a hill. Memory could say where it would go fast or slow, but the eyes couldn't guess.

For its own obscure reasons, the flamewall always moved quickly through this shallow valley. It would slow almost to a stop at the ridges above, as if considering, as if taking in the view. Then it would plunge down through the valley like an inundation, moving at the slow walking pace that was its maximum speed.

It was a dangerous spot, if you didn't know. But everyone knew. Everyone except the interlopers.

The flamewall was close enough that its light shone through the tent fabric. I put one hand over the snake on my arm. It was time to decide whether I wanted to die by dismemberment or end this life in the flames.

Servitor Graft

In the command tent, the Conquis began the meeting calmly, as though he had just boxed up an old pair of shoes instead of a living, breathing human.

"I want answers," the Conquis said. His staff were arrayed around the map table, their emotions divergent. The chief scientist seemed distracted; he had brought along Scitech Gustafsen, who appeared to be slightly nervous. The quartermaster meanwhile was scowling at nothing. And the lieutenant was absent, out in the dark somewhere trying to help some sentries reboot a night-vision smart system for which everyone—*everyone*—had forgotten the admin password.

The Conquis turned to his chief scientist. "Why haven't we received any messages from the bottleneck station? Where is my uranium? Why aren't the smart systems working, and why can't you remember how to fix them?" His eyes swept from person to person, seeking out the fuck-up, the one who should be punished.

"My conqueror," the chief began, "the injector is not like an elevator or a booster rocket. It did not *physically* move us into this world."

The Conquis's expression said, we're here, aren't we?

"Of course," the scientist continued, "we *exist* physically. We are not virtual. But we have been transferred into a completely different universe." He gestured to his left. "Dr. Gustafsen is our expert cosmologist."

Gustafsen stepped forward. "The answer to your questions has to do with the bottleneck station. And with the nature of our reality." He scanned the command tent for props and spotted some rolled-up napkins at the table where we had laid out cans of coffee.

He grabbed a cloth napkin and laid it out on the map table in the middle of the tent, pushing aside the tiny model drop-pods that had been at its center.

"This napkin," Dr. Gustafsen said, flattening the cloth out, "is like the fabric of our prime universe. When the Iter researchers—"

"The squatters," interrupted the chief scientist.

"When they were, ah, *hired* to create this realm by the Lord Commandant," Dr. Gustafsen continued, "they pinched off a bit of the prime universe." He demonstrated with his fingers, twisting a bit of the cloth into a little pouch. "And then, to make sure it wasn't merely an empty void, they *infused* it with matter-energy from the prime universe."

Gustafsen scanned around him again for a prop and plucked a whole walnut from its bowl on the side table. Then he tucked the walnut into the pouch in the napkin.

« One day your acorn will be planted. »

"It goes without saying, of course," said the chief scientist, "that this matter-energy was stolen from the People."

« Who stole it from the star of the Iter. »

The Conquis—who had himself taken a fistful of walnuts and

begun to crack them open with his bare hands—grunted for Gustafsen to continue.

"But to contain that energy and matter," Gustafsen said, "to keep it from spilling back out into the prime universe, they needed to separate the two. To tie off the bottleneck." With a piece of orange ribbon he produced from within his white jacket, he neatly tied it around the neck of the pouch containing the walnut and placed the napkin back on the table, gesturing as though he had just finished a magic trick. *Tada.*

"So, the ribbon is the bottleneck station," the Conquis concluded.

"Oh, no!" Gustafsen replied, and the chief cast him a sharp glance. "The Iter used the bottleneck station to fold spacetime, to infuse this pocket with energy and mass. But now that this universe is fully formed, it will continue to hold its own shape. Which is perhaps why the Iter—"

"The *squatters*," the chief interjected.

"—tried to blow up the bottleneck station. Or at least the injector," Gustafsen finished. "To keep from being followed."

"But we *did* follow them," the Conquis replied, impatient. A gust of wind outside shook the tent. The Conquis added, "Gentleman, we have a war to win. I don't have all night."

"Dr. Gustafsen," the chief replied, "is just about to answer your questions." The Conquis scowled and ate some of the nutmeat from a walnut he had cracked open.

"Yes, the big questions," Gustafsen said. "Where is the uranium? Why has data been changed or deleted? Why are there certain things we can't remember?"

He picked up a model of a drop-pod from the table and continued. "Once a pocket universe is formed, you can't merely pop a physical object into it." He pantomimed trying to push the drop-pod through the tied-off opening to the pouch in the napkin. "There's no physical tunnel. But there is an *informational* tunnel."

Gustafsen dropped his props back onto the table. "The injector at the bottleneck station can reduce a physical object—a person, a radio, a drop-pod—down to the minimum essential information needed to describe that thing. And then it sends that information here, into the pocket universe, where the object is remade. Regrown, almost. Condensed out of excess energy in *this* universe."

Most of the men at the table seemed uncomfortable with the idea. The Conquis glowered, but it wasn't clear if he was simply trying to understand the concept or was unsettled by the existential implications of what Gustafsen was saying.

« He's trying to figure out if he can use this information to kill something. »

Gustafsen glanced over at us, searching for a receptive face. We shifted our gaze to stare at our clasped hands, rubbing at an old scar on our left thumb where we had—

Where was the scar? We lifted our hands slightly to get better light. We'd had a ragged scar on our left thumb since childhood. We'd cut it badly on a sharp piece of debris not long after the People had arrived, and it hadn't healed properly. It had left a bulge of scar tissue over the knuckle.

Now that scar was gone.

"We have technology that does something similar," the chief scientist said, still addressing the Conquis. "Every time you send a message by video, that information is compressed into digital data and then reconstituted into visual form at the other end."

"Exactly," Gustafsen agreed, with a nod at the chief scientist. "But that information is also filtered on the way. Our computers perform error correction on the data to fix any transmission problems. And they check for viruses or malware and remove data that could be malicious in order to protect our systems. Before their work at the bottleneck station, many of the people you are seeking—Tycho and the others—were experts in information theory and had developed algorithms that could repair corrupted data or fill in missing packets."

"So, the injector did something to filter . . . *us?*" the Conquis asked, clearly disturbed by the notion. "When we came through?"

"I suspect it was the recipient that did the filtering," Gustafsen replied. "The pocket universe itself. A large amount of uranium, for example, could be considered dangerous."

"It *is* dangerous," the Conquis replied. "To them."

"As for missing information," Gustafsen said, "it could be simple over compression, like when a photograph is shrunk down to a smaller size and loses its fine detail."

« Wrong », an ancestor said flatly. « If information density were the issue, the Souven wouldn't work. »

The Conquis may have had the same thought, as his eyes shifted over to us and then back to the cosmologist. "Why would we lose only *some* information?"

« Why would you lose some memories but not others? »

"Lethologica," said Gustafsen, "is the feeling of having something on the tip of your tongue. A memory you can't quite access. The memories—"

The chief scientist jumped in before Gustafsen could continue. "It is impossible to say," he explained, "without investigating further."

The wind outside was growing. The tent fabric was flapping back and forth against the metal structure inside, as though the walls were panting.

"If filters stripped out potential malware from the incoming data stream," Gustafsen said, "they could have been overzealous. They could have removed anything that seemed dangerous, whether it was a radioactive element or a military algorithm or even a human memory of how to do something it deemed . . . harmful. The process may be baked into the structure of this universe."

« This universe will defend itself. »

"Will this affect the beacon?" the Conquis asked. "Is this why we haven't received any messages?"

The orange beacon stood still in its place next to the bowl of walnuts. Within a given universe it functioned merely as a sophisticated radio, broadcasting messages between ships or helping them to navigate. Between universes, the beacon could receive messages sent from the prime universe in the form of relativistic muon–anti-muon pairs. For this campaign, our beacons had also been modified with an emergency mode that could send a single message back to prime universe. But the act would burn them out—literally—and if you were within a hundred meters of the beacon when the message was sent, the shower of particles it produced in the process would triple your risk of dying from otherwise rare carcinomas.

"That's entirely possible," Dr. Gustafsen replied. "The barrier between universes is thinnest near this world's sun, where we arrived. We may be too far from the sun right now for the beacon to function properly. But ultimately, that is superficial. The real question is—"

But before he could finish, the lieutenant burst into the tent.

"Conquis!" he shouted. "We need you outside."

....

We exited the command tent, and the view outside was startling. The grassfire had somehow crossed the moat and entered the camp. We expected something ragged, more smoke than fire. But this fire was tall and bright, burning forward in a line as straight as a parade march.

From her prison tent nearby, the squatter girl was shouting at us to run. The Conquis ignored her.

The lieutenant reported, "Everyone except the sentries have taken shelter in the pods, my conqueror."

« Not everyone. »

The servitors were still hard at work, cooking food, repositioning equipment and supplies, using the jeeps to drag pallets of boxes and munitions away from the fire.

"The pod armor will protect from heat and flame," the Conquis agreed. At this, Gustafsen wandered off in the direction of one of the drop-pods. A moment later, the Conquis added, "But nevertheless have the servitors use fire suppressant to keep the flames away from our tents."

The lieutenant shouted instructions and the servitors began to spray portable fire extinguishers at the base of the flames nearby. As far as we could tell, this made no difference. A nearby light stand, powered by a thundering generator, was soon engulfed by the flames. Within the wall of fire, it shimmered and seemed to grow ragged before disappearing.

We grew nervous. The Conquis was speaking to the chief scientist about data filters and paid no attention to the details of the firefighting.

The scales of the drop-pods shimmered in the light of the fire. We could not understand how the flames continued to grow. The dry grass in the middle of camp had already been charred by the rocket engines when we landed; there shouldn't have been any fuel left to burn.

Still, the fires moved forward relentlessly. The first drop-pod they reached was now completely engulfed. We watched it through the flames. For a moment it seemed as if the pod were fluttering into pieces, as if its silver scales were dissolving.

An optical illusion, to be sure, caused by the reflection of bright light. We glanced at the Conquis for confirmation. He was staring at the pod, but we saw then that his pupils were so dilated by amphor that—who knows what he saw.

« Amphor is habit-forming », an ancestor warned. « Long term side-effects include dependency, brain damage, and irreversible psychosis. »

The lieutenant's eyes were sober and concerned as he lifted his radio. "Lander Seven, come in," he said. "Lander Seven, respond."

"It's just the fire," the chief said, as if that were reassurance. "Flames create a plasma that blocks radio signals, like during atmospheric re-entry."

« This is no ordinary fire. »

We glanced toward the command tent, where the Souven was tucked in its pouch under the pillow of our cot. The flames were a few minutes away from the tent but approaching quickly. The girl in the prison tent behind us was shouting and whistling in a language I couldn't follow.

A second pod was soon overtaken by flames. The lieutenant called on the radio: "Lander Five, status." The only response was a burst of intense and buzzing static. Beneath the noise, or perhaps through the armored hatch in the distance, we thought we heard a scream.

"Keep that tent safe!" the Conquis shouted at the servitors laboring near the command tent, spraying the fire ineffectually with extinguishers. "Do I have to do your fucking jobs for you?" He walked over and pulled an extinguisher from the hands of the nearest servitor.

The wall of fire moved inexorably across a third pod, and this time the lieutenant's radio crackled with a message from the pod's occupants: "Flames are coming through the bulkhead! Flames are coming through!"

"Evacuate the lander!" the lieutenant shouted into his radio. But the pod's only hatch was already covered in flame, the men inside trapped.

"Conquis!" the lieutenant yelled. The Conquis was distracted, shouting at servitors, spraying fire suppressant that seemed to do nothing. The lieutenant shouted into his radio, "All personnel, evacuate the pods!"

"No!" the Conquis shouted, dropping his empty fire extinguisher on the ground and turning back to his second-in-command. "We need those pods. Launch them!"

"Sir!" the lieutenant exclaimed. "We can't launch with people nearby." As they argued, soldiers had popped the hatches on nearby pods, boiling out like ants.

The Conquis grabbed the radio from the lieutenant's hand and called to the three pods furthest from the fire. "Lander One, Lander Four, Lander Nine! Lift off and find a new landing site!"

The lieutenant recoiled in horror. "There's no time for the pre-flight checklist!" he said. "And we have people out in the open!"

“Skip pre-flight checklist,” the Conquis relayed into the radio. “Start up the engines and go.”

Pandemonium overtook the camp. Servitors had given up fighting the fire and were hurriedly loading supplies onto jeeps or dragging them toward safety. Scitechs argued with the servitors, insisting their equipment be moved with care.

One of the pods at the far edge of camp lit up its engines. We covered our mouth reflexively, in fear of toxic propellant. The pod lifted slowly as the pilot tried to keep his exhaust plume to a moderate size. He got to a height of about fifty feet before one of its engines sputtered and the pod turned sideways and rocketed over the camp, into the wall of flame.

There was no crashing sound, no explosion. It was simply swallowed by fire.

The chaos around us seemed to accelerate. Perhaps it was the toxic propellant of the nearby engines, but we felt like we could barely breathe.

« The girl! »

« The Souven! »

The young woman had stopped shouting. Her prison tent had minutes, at most, before it was overtaken.

“Graft!” shouted the Conquis. “Secure my gear!” We froze. He was helping to load a crate of munitions onto a jeep, his back turned to us. Beside us, the flames had reached the command tent.

We ran inside. One corner had been engulfed in flames already, and the foot of our cot was being devoured.

« The Souven, now! » our ancestors insisted. We rushed to our cot and dragged it out of the flames. The far end of the cot was not burned but simply gone.

We reached under our pillow and found the Souven, safe and

intact, along with our acorn sealed in resin. We tucked them into our tunic, then grabbed what we could find of the Conquis's personal effects, stuffing them into duffel bags. His toiletries. Spare clothing. We grabbed his case of amphor on the table and then reached for the bright orange beacon beside it.

« Leave it. »

We grasped one of the beacon's many handles.

« Just leave it there! »

The tent walls began to collapse around us as the corner-posts were devoured. Disregarding the urgings of our ancestor, we took the beacon. It was almost too much to carry, but we strapped the beacon over one shoulder, a duffel onto our back, and another heavy bag of clothing onto our front. We exited the doorway but couldn't see the Conquis. There was distant shouting from the dark, "Essential equipment this way!"

A second pod lifted off, engines on full. The plume of exhaust flattened the enormous kitchen tent, which had been full of servitors and sent out a wide plume of dust and debris that engulfed us. For a moment, we couldn't see anything.

« The girl! »

We stumbled toward her prison tent, wiping grit from our eyes. We pushed through the door and felt a powerful blow against our front. If it weren't for the bag of clothing strapped across us, we surely would have cracked a rib.

"Oh, it's you!" she said, wide-eyed. "Sorry for kicking you."

"The camp is being evacuated," we said. She turned toward the cargo strap on her arm, angry and fearful. "It's fake," we said, and reached out. She flinched back, grimacing, her arm held away from her body, as we released the catch on the strap.

It fell to the ground. "I'm not coming with you," she said.

"Everyone is distracted," we answered. "Run fast. Don't stop for anything."

She seemed surprised for a moment that we were helping her escape. She took a step forward, ready to sprint, and then paused. "Come with me."

This world had been full of surprises, but that was the first time we were truly shocked.

"Come with me to the Ami," she said, "and you'll never have to eat dirt."

The offer was so unexpected we could barely make sense of it in the moment.

"We can't," we answered. "We have duties."

She frowned sadly but didn't argue. "Wind at your back," she said. And then she sprinted through the door of the tent.

Char of the Ami

I ran as fast as I could. I passed a huge, flattened tent. Caught a glimpse of a man in red, struggling to get out of its wreckage. I wanted to stop, but I followed Graft's instructions: I ran and thought only of speed.

Within seconds I had passed the perimeter of the camp. After a minute of frantic running, my lungs felt like they were burning. I had to slow from an all-out sprint to a fast jog.

Doing my best to keep pace, I ran alongside the flamewall. I hoped the intruders would be moving away from it.

The flamewall was to my right. In the rush to escape, I had ended up running east. Away from the Ami and toward the forest.

I must have gone three kilometers before my shaking legs grew clumsy. I tripped on a tree root where grassland gave way to forest and tumbled to the ground.

Wincing, I breathed through gritted teeth. I had skinned an elbow and perhaps a knee. I rolled up into a sitting position, clutching my left elbow, feeling blood and dirt against my right palm.

Looking back at the interloper camp, my heart pounding, I saw one of the silver not-fish lift up into the starlit sky, propelled on its own pillar of flame.

It was only then that I thought of Tycho.

Servitor Graft

The pell-mell escape was fear, confusion, exhaustion. The servitors had largely managed the evacuation on their own, moving supplies in jeeps or on their backs, charting a path through the dark that ended in a copse of trees a safe distance—we hoped—from the burning flames.

We stopped finally there to breathe, collapsing onto our side beneath a massive oak. We had not even had time to drink water before the Conquis demanded amphor.

He was surrounded by a knot of soldiers and Scitechs. "Conquis, that was no ordinary grassfire," said one of the panting scientists.

« Stating the obvious, as usual. » We pushed through the cluster to offer a glass of amphor to the Conquis. He was breathing hard, and we could hear the wheezing of his battle-scarred alveoli.

Instead of gulping down the amphor he sipped it between ragged gasps.

The Conquis waved away the men surrounding him. "Give him space," we demanded, impertinent but they listened despite our low rank.

Even in the dim illumination of the jeep's headlights, we could see the fear in his eyes. We knew what he was thinking: that any of us had survived was a goddamned miracle.

The "grassfire" had burned through the armored drop-pods like they were papier-mâché. With flames at our backs, we had been forced to rush through unknown and dark terrain teeming with enemies. If the squatters had been ruthless, they could have surrounded the camp, picked off the soldiers as they fled the burning drop-pods or set up an ambush full of traps in the dark.

No matter their level of technology, the squatters could simply have sprung at us from the dark with heavy rocks and sharp sticks, could have bludgeoned the overloaded servitors and confused technicians. But they didn't. They had spared us. Why?

Perhaps because of the hissing, breathing box piled onto a jeep along with crates of ammunition and disposable dinnerware.

"The hostage," murmured the Conquis, between sips of amphor. We had been following exactly his train of thought.

« The Souven stimulates cognitive empathy », an ancestor warned. « It's dangerous to use around people like him. »

We had soaked up the conqueror's way of thinking, no doubt. How else could we have stayed safe and alive? But our hyperempathy aside, the Conquis was wrong. It was not the presence of a hostage, spray-foamed into a metal cage. The reason was much simpler. « The Ami are gentle. »

And now those of us who remained were in a grove of trees some kilometers away from the fire.

The fact that the host of survivors and equipment had been able to move so quickly to these trees was not the result of logistic mastery—it was because almost all of the equipment and supplies had burned up. There was very little left to carry. The few cargo jeeps were full of whatever gear could be hastily jammed into them. The rest had been rescued by servitors who had marched into the dark with heavy bags on their backs and strapped across their shoulders. The soldiers had been occupied pointing their guns at the shadows and had done little to help.

« The precious Souven is intact. Our cultural memory is intact. That's all that matters. »

Now the servitors sprawled on the ground, chests heaving, eyes closed. Overall, REPO's numbers had been cut in half. But at a glance we could see that almost every servitor had survived. In contrast, the soldiers who had bravely "stood their ground" at their stations inside the armored drop-pods had been engulfed by fire. But the servitors, exposed or huddled in tents, had no choice but to keep moving as the flames approached. And now we servitors made up more than half of all the survivors. Under their exhaustion, we could sense their horror and even anger. Most were not used to combat—they had been conscripted from the servitor pool on the bottleneck station, not already inured to violence through personal servitude like ourself.

Above us, the pulsating stars had collected at one of the polar oceans, looking like wriggling fireflies being washed down a sink, disappearing one by one into the center of the concave sea.

At the opposite end of the world, the sun began to rise. No—rise isn't the right word. A whirling sandstorm at one pole of the world began to glow, and then a lustrous yellow orb slowly pushed through the cloud of sand until it was fully emerged. The sun actually seemed to brighten, to shift from hues of deep yellow to white as it slid along an invisible axis between the east and west poles.

We survivors and our equipment were soon dappled with the dawn light that passed through the foliage above. But the angle of the sunlight was eerie—it was not the soft sideways light of a planetary dawn. We were so close to the west pole that the light came almost straight down on us.

We looked out through the tree branches toward the ocean. Yesterday, we glimpsed several unfamiliar birds we couldn't recognize. But knowledge from the Souven had passed into our mind during the brief sleep the Conquis had interrupted. Now, over the strange sea, we spotted Caspian terns, gulls, puffins, cormorants, pelicans, skuas, and in the distance a shape—impossibly—like an albatross.

The Conquis beckoned his surviving command staff to him. The amphor seemed to have improved his breathing. "Thank the Forefathers that we had a prisoner to keep the squatters from attacking us," he said.

The lieutenant, his face smeared with ash, nodded in grim agreement. "To protect ourselves, we need more hostages."

"We showed them mercy," said the Conquis, "and see how they repaid us. It's time to stop being gentle with these savages."

Chapter 5

Retaliation

Char of the Ami

Even in our cozy microcosm, moving from Germinal's grasslands to the forest was like going from one universe to another. The dry, matted grass beneath my feet gave way to a carpet of moss that was thicker and softer than the rug in my grandmother's wagon. As I walked, the dawn sky above was gently obscured first by boughs of birch and elm, then hidden completely by a continuous canopy of enormous fir and cedar trees.

The warm wind of the open plain gave way to air that was calm, cool, and humid. The odor of ash and dead bison had faded, replaced by the rich scent of humus and the sharp, resinous blend of a dozen kinds of conifer.

I had walked barely five minutes into the forest—limping slightly from my tumble—before I encountered the giant owl.

The giant owl was, of course, a human dressed as an owl, whose job as the "Friendly Watcher" was to welcome visitors and to keep eyes out for trouble.

Trouble had found all of us.

When I reported to her what had happened—a short summary that left out some painful details—the first thing she offered me was a hug. I took it. She was a friendly, well-rounded woman older than I, and as soon as she enfolded me in her warm arms and her feathery cloak, I began to cry—a reaction to comfort after adversity.

The Friendly Watcher comforted me for a few minutes, offered some chocolate and snacks she dug up from a cache at a nearby cedar tree, and then invited me to join her on the high walk. "A lot has happened," she said. "Our people want to talk to you, if you're willing." I agreed. She made a few hooting calls up into the canopy overhead and far away someone answered.

I followed her deeper into the forest. As we moved away from the grasslands, the trees got bigger. On the Ami circuit, our tallest tree was some thirty meters, but that was easily overshadowed by the forest's massive redwoods and firs.

As we walked, and the full-body shock of the escape began to diminish, I started to feel more subtle and specific sensations. A burning on my left elbow, where I had skinned it. An odd twinge in my right ankle, where perhaps I had rolled it. And a churning high in my abdomen, almost inside my ribs. Hunger? No.

Shame. I was ashamed to have been tricked by Conquis, to have stayed in that tent out of fear an innocuous object would cut my arm off. I'd been used as bait to lure Tycho in, and I'd failed to warn him of the danger of the intruders. And when Tycho had been trapped in that box and the camp was overtaken by the flamewall, I had run without even stopping to check on him.

For all I knew, the intruders had left him behind inside that box. For all I knew, Tycho had already passed into the next life.

If I had been at home, I would have spoken to my grandmother. She knew something about shame, about leaving someone behind. And she knew the difference between guilt and shame, a distinction that eluded me in the moment. Even my parents would have been helpful had they not been on a Tapestry mission to the desert.

I began to hear the sounds of work ahead, the chopping of wood. We were deep inside the forest.

....

The trees above were so tall that a person who fell from the top would be able to recite the entire sunset prayer before they struck the ground.

Their forest's patterns of growth were not entirely natural. The branches of nearby trees had become deliberately entangled, braided and plaited together in complex structural patterns. Each passing of the flamewall strengthened them, helped them to grow, tightened the weavings further. Together this latticework of living branches formed a series of bridges and promenades—the "high walk"—which could hold the weight of many humans but would flex and bend with the swaying of enormous trees.

"You can walk a third of the way around the world and never touch the ground," the owl explained. "In another five generations, the high walk will circle the whole of Germinal."

"It's beautiful," I said, pausing to admire the diffuse sunlight that passed through the verdant canopy above. "But why?"

"What better way to spend a life," she said, "than to make something both beautiful and useful?" After a moment, she added. "It's a great circle to echo the circles of the world. The work of generations connects us to our ancestors and to our descendants." She frowned, then added, "And when the uninvited guests arrive, I would much rather be up there than on the forest floor."

We approached an enormous fir tree that was encircled by a flattened helix of branches serving as a spiral staircase. The shape was clearly artificial. Like our buffet trees at home, the branches had been placed by flame-grafting. Many autumns past, someone had neatly removed small branches from some other tree, sliced open a patch of bark on this giant, and then pressed the branches into the cleft. When the flamewall passed, it had healed the wound, rerouted tiny vessels of xylem and phloem in the tree to form something that was good as new.

It worked on trees but not on humans.

The Friendly Watcher and I ascended the spiral steps—there was no handrail around the staircase, so I kept one shoulder close to the tree trunk as we climbed. My host seemed oblivious to the danger of falling, striding near the outside of the spiral where the branches were thinner, where they bent and sprung back with each of her steps.

Once we reached a nexus of bridges above, finally enclosed by living branches that served as a balustrade, I paused to look down and catch my breath. An ivory-billed woodpecker flew past. Below us, a young woman with a sharp ax was chopping away each branch of the stairway, leaving nothing behind that could be climbed.

My host sighed. "We'll be using rope ladders for a year or two," she said. "But it will keep us safe until we can deal with this problem."

....

The high walk was wide enough for five people to stand abreast.

Taut strings ran along the outside of the railings, to carry messages along the length of the high walk. The Forest People were not content to send messages via bike courier like the Grasslanders or whistle across distances like the Ternfolk. A network of "Helpful Listeners" were arrayed at bridge intersections throughout their entire territory, listening for messages through the strands, plucking messages out to other Listeners to pass on.

I expected that, by now, half of those Listeners already knew that an Ami had been captured by the interlopers, escaped, and was on her way to—what, a meeting?

Breakfast, it turned out. There was a little cul-de-sac off the walkway ahead and I could already smell the food they had laid out. Fried mushrooms and rice. Berry salad. Pinenut pudding. Even a few short skewers of roasted bison meat—though the Forest People were famously sparing with animal protein.

There was enough food laid out to feed at least a dozen people, though only four were waiting to welcome me. As they invited me to take a seat among a pile of cushions, it became clear that *all* the food was for me, so that I might choose first what I liked. They offered me a warm towel to wash my face and hands. It smelled of citrus as I wiped the grime from my cheeks.

My owl escort gave the four others assembled a brief summary of what happened and then she introduced each one to me. A heart-holder, clad in blue. A Helpful Listener, lithe fingers poised on the wires beside us. A medic with a bag stuffed full of dressings. And an elderly conciliator, dressed hastily in ceremonial garb.

The heart-holder spoke first. "We are so sorry about how they treated you." Her warm eye contact was a balm for my spirit. "You did nothing to deserve such disrespect or to be threatened in that way."

I thanked her, and she continued. "You are safe here with us, and we will do our best to take care of you. Please eat. May our medic tend to your injury?"

I nodded and the medic approached to kneel beside me. Asking my permission, he gently daubed my scraped left elbow with a warm, wet cloth with a strong scent of rosemary.

With my free right hand, I put some mushrooms in my mouth—they melted like butter. The medic began to wrap my elbow in gauze. I had the impression that if I'd asked them to, I would have been fed by hand, too, while the medic cared for my scrapes and washed my hands and feet. It was tempting.

"Char, how are you feeling right now?" the heart-holder asked.

"I'm worried about my uncle," I answered. Which was true but vastly oversimplified. Emotions rippled through my body like a tired and churning sun at the end of its day. "And I'm worried for anyone else who might encounter those people."

"Do you think they are dangerous to everyone?" she asked. "Could this be another Blue Moon Brawl?"

In that moment I thought back to Violet, how she pretended to be a handfish prying open the shell of a clam to devour it. The Conquis wanted to do that to Germinal. It made me afraid for the children—for all of us.

"Worse. They claim we are here wrongfully," I said. "They say they want to take the entire world."

The conciliator nodded at the Listener, who plucked at the strings sending messages through the forest.

"We need to rescue my uncle," I said.

"Discussions have begun," the heart-holder assured me. "After the airboats arrived, your Uncle Tycho came here along with two Grasslanders to ask us to mobilize. He told us about the, ah, *unexpected* request for help from the Spring People. We Forest People began preliminary discussions on whether to intercede. He grew . . . frustrated with the timetable once he heard of your capture and left while consultations were still underway."

I nodded.

"Those discussions are now more than eight percent complete," the heart-holder continued. "Quite fast, under the circumstances. Once your uncle left, a runner arrived sent by Red Grandma, calling for an emergency meeting on the Ami circuit in spring, this afternoon."

"The Forest People will attend?"

"It's under discussion," she answered. "At the very least, we will contribute a full meal, friendship wraps included. But right now, I'm worried about *you*. You've been through a stressful, frightening experience. I want to give you a chance to talk about what happened, to feel safe. When we respond to stress in a timely way, we can keep it from becoming chronic."

"But why is he here?" I asked, tilting my head at the conciliator.

"I want you to know," the heart-holder said, "that you don't have to do anything you don't feel comfortable with. You can stay here as long as you want. You don't have to do anything that would make you feel anxious or fearful." But her response—the way she talked about anxiety without answering my question—made my heart thump in my chest and my mouth go dry. I took a long sip of friendship tea; it tasted like bitter licorice, but it helped me relax.

Then I made eye contact with the conciliator, who spoke for the first time, his voice like smooth river stones rattling in a leather bag. "A kind of airboat belonging to the newcomers fell into the forest overnight," he explained softly. "They crashed by accident, we think. Most of them survived.

"You are the Habitant who has spent the most time with these people," he said. "If you feel up to it, you can help us talk to them."

Servitor Graft

The Conquis wasted no time. Despite the fact that nearly half the soldiers had been lost—lowering their total numbers from fifty to less than thirty—he ordered six fire teams to spread out in all directions from the grove we occupied. Their orders were to find squatters and to take hostages by any means necessary.

We wanted nothing more than a few hours' rest with the Souven. If we could strengthen our memories of our ancestors, we could overcome some of the nauseated disorientation we felt in every moment since our arrival. And perhaps remember something that would help keep us alive in this strange world. The memories written to our neurons by the Souven's magnetic induction could feel more enduring and more vivid than things we experienced with our own senses, and we yearned for that respite.

Instead of granting us rest, however, the Conquis assigned us to help the lieutenant take inventory of what had survived. The quartermaster, who had sheltered in a drop-pod with other officers, had not survived the arrival of the flamewall. Perhaps, given the Conquis's anger over the disastrous state of our remaining supplies, the quartermaster had gotten off easy.

"Helping" the lieutenant with inventory meant taking inventory ourself. The lieutenant was preoccupied—he spent hours calling on the radio that morning, trying to reach other survivors. At first there had been genuine hope that some of the drop-pods overrun by flames might have survived, that their armor had protected them. The flame wall didn't even seem that *hot*, especially compared with the superheated re-entry plasma the drop-pods could endure.

But it grew clear that six pods—those that had remained grounded at the landing zone—were simply gone. We could not yet peer over the top of the flamewall to survey the site, but if the flames kept moving at their constant crawling pace, in a few days we might be able to see over them, across the curving world, and see what remained of the pods.

« You will see nothing but green grass. »

Of the three pods that had lifted off, we could reach only one. The first had crashed into the flames after launch. The second, which had flattened our kitchen tent as it took off, had crash-landed on a rocky plateau near the ocean, perhaps thirty kilometers away. They answered their radio and were in communication but were completely out of fuel—hence the hard landing.

The third craft, according to the pilot of the second, had been trying to find a safe place to land but for reasons unknown had plunged into dense forest and stopped responding.

So, the entirety of REPO had only a single drop-pod remaining, and it couldn't even launch. At least it still had its beacon intact. Including the one we had rescued from that command tent, however, that left only two beacons. This left the Conquis with a way to punch through the barrier between universes, to send messages—one per beacon—back to the cosmos we came from. But in doing so, each transmitter would burn itself out in the shower of exotic particles it created. The Conquis would need to bide his time until he knew for certain what messages he wanted to send.

In the absence of the quartermaster, *we* took inventory. We had no training as a quartermaster, but enough of our ancestors had been logisticians that we could count boxes. And we could read.

Still, reading produced moments of confusion. A bundle containing a tent was labeled "Size: 4-man. Colour: Green." *Colour*. With a "u," which was not how the People spelled it. That must have been a typo from the factory.

« It's not a typo from the factory. »

Out of habit, we rubbed the spot on our left thumb where we'd once had a thick scar, though it had vanished when we came into this world. Then we got back to our task.

In the end, we cataloged the contents of three cargo jeeps full of heavy supplies. The first two were packed with bedrolls and tents for all of the soldiers—rather in excess of what we needed, given the warm weather and recent events—and pallets of bottled water. With the plentiful streams around us, this, too, seemed unnecessary.

The third jeep contained two crates of ammunition, a box of disposable dinnerware, and a foam-filled cage the size of a small coffin that hissed and sputtered. It also carried an assortment of heavy scientific equipment that the Scitechs had unloaded and were now putting to use.

One important thing was missing: food.

From some of the other servitors we learned that they had begun loading food into the third jeep—the other two having been loaded, sensibly, with shelter and water—but the chief scientist had interrupted them and insisted on their loading up mass spectrometers, carbon-dating equipment, and other expensive pieces of machinery instead.

When we relayed this fact to the Conquis, who was examining a crude, hand-drawn map beneath a pop-up canopy a quarter of the size of his former command tent, he was less angry than we expected.

"We will take food from the squatters soon enough," he said. "Or shoot animals to eat."

"There is only one beacon with us," we added. "And one more at the crash-landed pod ahead." The Conquis frowned deeply at this. Hungry servitors didn't bother him. But we needed a beacon to guide the arrival of the Commandant's ship. Since the act of sending a message back to the prime universe would burn out a beacon, we had to be careful. With only two beacons available, we could only send one message, assuming we wanted to keep one beacon intact with which to receive messages.

"The Lord Commandant will bring a spare beacon when he arrives," the Conquis replied. But he did order us to fetch the chief to give an update.

"Things are going well with our investigations," the chief began once he arrived; it was such a bald-faced lie, given our collective circumstances, that we almost laughed, but he continued. "We were able to salvage the vital equipment we need to investigate this world and will have results within the hour."

"I'm still awaiting answers from Gustafsen," the Conquis answered.

The chief grimaced. "From what we can tell, Gustafsen was on board the drop-pod that crashed in the forest," he said. "But he can be . . . independently minded almost to the point of insubordination. We may be better off without him."

"If he is insubordinate," the Conquis said, "why did you choose to bring him?"

"He was the only specialist on the bottleneck station," the chief shrugged. "We go to war with the people we have, not the ones we wish we had. But it's a moot point. Once we have the measurements we need, we'll be able to take full control of this world."

"The supply caches our soldiers have been digging up," the Conquis said. "What do you make of them? Is there a factory underground? An automated delivery system?"

The chief scientist shifted, uncomfortable. "We've found dozens of underground caches but no sign of delivery tubes. The caches have intact root systems growing all around them, as if they've been in place for years. And this world is completely empty of the manufacturing byproducts that accumulate in most habs over time. No PCBs, no PFAS, no microplastics."

The Conquis made a reasonable leap, "Is this nanotechnology?"

«This is way beyond nanotechnology. Nanotech is like a pottery wheel compared to this.»

Before the chief scientist could answer, a nervous younger Scitech approached, holding a tablet at arms-length in front of him as if it were a pot of sizzling oil.

"Conquis, Chief," the Scitech said, "there's something you need to know."

Char of the Ami

The crashed airboat—what the intruders called a drop-pod—was only a few kilometers away. We followed the high walk there and the Friendly Watchers asked us to stay quiet as we traveled. Warnings had spread along the wires that interlopers had entered the forest and were chasing its residents. The Forest People were retreating from the grassland borders, hiding deeper in the trees and the mountains. Periodically, we heard rattling and rapid bangs in the distance, like fireworks.

The drop-pod had come down through thick foliage, snapping branches as it tumbled to the ground, and finally coming to rest in a dense patch of ferns.

I turned to the Forest conciliator. "Their dialect is like the ceremonial tongue," I said to prepare him, "with a strange accent."

He frowned. "Odd that they would speak something so archaic," he said. "But it *is* the language we have in common. Using it will be good practice for the next Convergence."

There had been four people on board the drop-pod. One of them—a soldier—had been seriously injured in the crash and was in the process of dying from a head injury. Forest medics had tried to rush him to the autumn flamewall to send him into the next life—the Forest People believed it would give a child bad memories if the body died before it reached the flamewall—but the other survivors from the drop-pod had objected. So, the soldier lay unconscious on a cloth stretcher, the time between each gasping breath growing longer by the minute.

The other three survivors were in much better shape. The pilot stared silently toward the stretcher, his ashen faced racked with guilt. A servitor in maroon sat among the ferns near the capsule, face turned up in disbelief at the huge trees above. And a white-clad Scitech was talking with a few of the Friendly

Watchers and armed Grasslanders who surrounded the site in a loose circle.

The Scitech smiled through his obvious fear, and it struck me that a human being dressed as an owl could seem either very cuddly or very intimidating, depending on the circumstances.

As I approached, the scientist made eye contact with me and called out. "I'm so sorry for what happened to you and your friend," he said. "That was hard to watch." He tried to step toward me, but an owl raised a wing to keep him in place.

"He is my *uncle*," I corrected him. "Or was."

"He still is," the man said. "I watched the servitors load him up and drive him to safety." Sheepishly, he added, "Well, drive him away somewhere, at least."

I felt cautious relief then. "I am Char," I told him. "I am called 'She Who Seeks Justice.'"

"Uh, I am Doctor Exeter Gustafsen," he replied, then rattled off a string of letters that meant nothing to me. Perhaps he expected me to be impressed, and when my face showed I wasn't, he added, "People call me Gus. I study universes."

The conciliator beside me stepped forward. "Why are you here?"

"I'm here because the People called!" he answered, in an oddly jocular voice. "And when the People call, you answer. That is, if you care about your career. Or your life!"

"You didn't have a choice?" asked the conciliator.

"I had the option of the injector or the airlock, if you call that a choice."

The conciliator glanced at me in confusion. I shrugged. I was getting used to their odd accent, but the vocabulary of the interlopers was foreign and often baffling.

"Did they threaten you with the armband?" I asked the man.

"Something like that," he replied. I stepped closer to look into his eyes, to see if he was being honest. "The Conquis is a ruthless man but a pussycat next to the Commandant."

"The leaders," I whispered to the conciliator, though he had already inferred the same.

The servitor, who had been listening to the conversation, spoke up then. "The Commandant's heart is evil, and his mind is filled only with hate."

"Keegan is right," Gus agreed, nodding at the man who'd just spoken.

"I would speak with these men," the conciliator said, "in the hope of regaining peace."

"That's a bad idea, brother," Gus replied. "You can't trust a word they say. They'll tell you anything if they think it will get them what they want."

"What do they want?" the conciliator asked.

"Everything," Gus said, waving his arms above himself. "They think this entire universe belongs to them. The Conquis is going to try to take control by force and pass it over to the Commandant. And then the Commandant will summon hundreds of soldiers—or thousands—until this world belongs to them."

Again, the conciliator and I exchanged a worried glance. To Gus, I said, "I only saw a few dozen soldiers at the camp."

"The rest are waiting in prime universe," he said. "For the signal to invade. If those guys activate a beacon, you're finished."

"How do we stop this beacon?" I asked.

"You've got to neutralize them as quickly as possible. Before you are overrun."

"What does this mean?" the conciliator asked. "'Neutralize'?"

The scientist seemed surprised. "Well, it means you've got to find their soldiers right now," he said, "and isolate them, take them prisoner, or kill them."

Servitor Graft

When the scientists departed, we were too stunned to speak. *The carbon isotopes we've found do not match the expected age of this universe.* That's what the nervous Scitech had said. For us, the news was a bombshell.

The chief scientist blustered, then. Promised to investigate further. Babbled about "time synchronization," then left. And the Conquis turned back to his map, seemingly unaware that something monumental had transpired.

« Time moves differently here », an ancestor explained, but it was stating the obvious. We could see clearly—from the mature forests and thick topsoil—that more than a few days had elapsed since this world was created. More even than a few weeks or months. « More than years », the ancestors insisted. « Centuries. A millennium! »

We needed to handle this delicately. To make the Conquis feel stupid was to provoke him.

"Could it be, Conquis," we ventured, "that a great deal of time has passed within this microcosm?"

"Of course," he said, dismissively. "This Tycho is now an old man. The squatters have wasted years in this place, and they are now old and weak."

« They have gotten soft. » We nodded at the Conquis in agreement, though he was staring in another direction. Our mind was noisy. « It has been generations! » We shook our head as if that would silence them.

We continued gently, "But you speak as if you have some deeper understanding that you have not yet been willing to share." His head didn't move, but his eyes snapped over to ours.

« Careful. Danger. » We bowed our head a few degrees and proceeded cautiously.

"When you captured the squatter Tycho," we said, "we know you noted the discrepancies. His height. The color of his eyes. You stayed calm before the men, as always, but we saw you wrinkle your nose; you smelled something was off."

The Conquis narrowed his eyes. "You are observant, Graft."

« You are, my child, but not for the reason he thinks. Keep going. »

"We realized—from your expression—that the prisoner didn't match the description," we said. "We saw you understand that this Tycho is not merely old, he is a different person entirely." The Conquis widened his eyes, threateningly.

« Don't make him feel a fool! »

We spoke quickly to rush past the moment of danger. "We know you glimpsed something then that you've been holding back," we said. "You didn't want to panic the men. But you've seen all the pieces—the biodiversity here, the cultural shift, the changes of accent and language—you've seen how it adds up. The look on your face told us that the time that has passed here has been much longer than the scientists first guessed."

« Yes, good. Blame the scientists. »

« Stop beating around the bush! He's getting impatient. »

"You understood," I prompted, "that the time that has passed has been longer than years even."

"Yes . . ." he said, his brows raised in sudden epiphany. "It's been decades!"

« He's a fucking idiot. »

"Well, yes, decades at first," we nodded. "And then . . ."

His face went blank for a moment then genuine understanding. "My Forefathers . . ." he gasped. And finally, a flicker of fear. We knew from experience how quickly fear could boil into rage.

« Move on! Redirect. »

"Thank you for helping us all to understand," we said, "that the traitors have squatted here for hundreds of years. Truly their crimes are beyond measure."

"Justice will be done," he answered reflexively. His eyes flicked back and forth with internal calculations. Existential questions were often beyond him, but his tactical mind was sharp. He would understand the strategic implications.

"If we call for reinforcements from the bottleneck station," he says, "it could take them a week to prepare and reach the injector. With the time slippage . . ."

Our ancestors were already doing the calculations. « Assuming a time ratio of roughly one day per century . . . »

We paraphrased for the Conquis, "In the eight days it took us to repair the injector, perhaps eight centuries passed here. At a rate of one century per day, our reinforcements won't arrive for another seven hundred years."

The Conquis seemed genuinely shaken, staring into the middle distance.

"The good news is that the Commandant's ship was already

being loaded to the injector as we were leaving," we added. "So, if they were quick enough to activate it after a few minutes, the Commandant could arrive within days."

« If they weren't quick, it could be months . . . »

The Conquis said nothing for a long few minutes. His face was taut. "Leave me, Graft," he said finally.

We did.

Char of the Ami

"Never have I met someone so bloodthirsty," the conciliator declared after we had walked some distance from the crash site. "Imagine meeting a stranger and inciting them to murder before even telling them the name of your mother!"

"Compared to the Conquis," I said, "this one seems like a peaceful man." The conciliator only shook his head in sad and silent disbelief.

The heart-holder, walking quietly alongside us, wasn't concerned with diplomatic propriety. "How are you doing, Char?"

It was impossible for me to answer succinctly. I felt dizzy, reeling. My uncle was alive—probably. The Conquis was a practiced liar. These things reduced, if only slightly, my shame at abandoning Tycho, at being so easily fooled. But Gus's strange behavior was even more baffling.

"I want to go home," I said, simply. My chest ached for the company of other Ami. I wanted to eat fruit, and gaze over the ocean and be rid of all these strange people. But if Gus were telling the truth, there was no safe place to retreat to.

"It's dangerous right now. The interlopers have sent out groups of men to chase us. Fortunately, the Grasslanders have already offered to escort you home," the heart-holder said, gesturing at a pair of mud-spattered riders a few strides away, "along with a few other people who will attend the emergency meeting." I nodded, and she beckoned the riders forward.

I already knew Boudica, the taller of the two, before she spoke. "I owe you an apology," she said. "I brought your uncle to the camp last night. I shouldn't have let him go down alone."

"It's not your fault," I told her. "You couldn't have stopped him. I forgive you."

"I'm grateful," Boudica said. Then she reached to her belt, pulled her trowel from its holster, and handed it to me. "I want you to have this," she said. "I know interlopers stole your trowel."

Her Grasslander trowel was different from the Ami style—it was longer and pointier, meant to cut through thick prairie turf. The butt of its weathered wooden handle was carved into the shape of a bison head. It was a beautiful piece that she had clearly carried for many years, and I tried politely to refuse. But she insisted.

"I'll feel better knowing that you are carrying it," Boudica told me. "I've got a spare." Then she hesitated for just a moment and continued, "My son Aden and I have a favor to ask."

The heart-holder stepped forward. "Char has been through enough today," she said. "Now she must rest and be safe."

I put an appreciative hand on the heart-holder's arm but turned again to the tall Grasslander and her son beside her. "What can I give you?"

"Knowledge," Boudica replied. "We have heard that their leader is a liar. But we heard it from the mouth of a would-be killer. Is there any interloper we can trust to tell the truth?"

I bowed my head thoughtfully. "Graft, perhaps. I don't think he is there willingly. He's a servant, dressed all in red."

The two Grasslanders met each other's eyes. Then Aden said, "If he is there unwillingly, we can rescue him. But many of the interlopers are dressed in red. Could you point him out to us?"

I nodded, but the heart-holder spoke up again. "It's too much to ask of her."

"If she could help bring peace," said the conciliator, "her risk may be worth it."

"I'm right here!" I snapped, more sharply than I had meant to. "If that's what must be done, fine: let's go get Graft."

....

Our departure took longer than I had hoped. The mother-and-son Grasslanders were eager to leave, but the Forest People were still involved in a lengthy discussion process over the wires. They hadn't yet committed to attending the emergency meeting in a formal diplomatic sense, but in the end, their gravel-voiced conciliator and the heart-holder offered to travel with us.

There had also been a commotion in the spring-most parts of the Forest lands. According to the Friendly Listeners, since yesterday *all* the cradles emerging from the spring flamewall had been full. It had never happened before that so many babies had come at once.

I thought of Quang Duc, the purple-eyed baby. Something terrible must have happened to the Spring People.

One last delay came when the scientist Gus and the servitor named Keegan asked if they could also join the meeting. It felt unprecedented, but there was no precedent for anything we were doing, so we agreed. Together we left, walking in a group and carrying the packages of food the Forest People had prepared, traveling west almost silently toward the edge of the forest.

We had nearly reached the grasslands when a polyphonic moan began to swell from the distance. The conciliator and the heart-holder stopped in their tracks.

"What is it?" whispered Gus.

"The wailing horn," I whispered back. "A Forest Person has died." But the sound continued, growing louder and more dissonant. "Multiple Forest People," I corrected myself.

The interlopers had done something terrible—that was apparent. Our two Forest companions looked heartbroken. "We'll have to catch up with you later," the heart-holder said. As she and the conciliator turned toward the road back, Gus stammered out an awkward condolence that was more like an apology.

The Grasslanders led us forward to the edge of the forest, where we crouched behind a hedge of highbush cranberry, weighted down with ripe fruit. A few other Grasslanders were waiting for us there with their tandem bicycles.

"The interlopers have been traveling near the coast," Boudica told us, using the soft Grasslander tongue. "One of their airboats landed on the Amber Moon like a bird with a broken leg. We think the others are trying to get to it. They have dispersed teams of hunters to search for us. Their main group is leapfrogging between groves of trees as they move, along with three self-propelled wagons. We think they are trying to hide, but they're incredibly loud all the time."

"Could you get close enough to see my uncle?" I asked.

She shook her head. "We think he's in a box in one of the wagons, which are always guarded. But we can draw hunters away from the group. Every time their hunters see a Grasslander on a bicycle, they give charge. They are like angry bulls."

"What is she saying?" Gus asked.

I switched back to the ceremonial tongue. "She thinks the Grasslanders can trick the interlopers into spreading out, so we can get to Graft."

"How can I help?" Gus said.

"You can travel separately," Boudica told him. "And stay out of the way."

If the distrust of the Grasslanders stung Gus, he didn't show it.

"We'll split up here," Boudica said. "My son will take Gus and Keegan to the meeting place while my brothers and sisters will scatter the interlopers. And I will sneak you close enough to find Graft. Are you ready?"

"No," I smiled tightly. "But I'll do it anyway."

Servitor Graft

After the Conquis dismissed us, we went to find a place to rest.

There were paths here, running alongside the coast, so firm and smooth that it was as if they had been paved. We walked along one of the paths in the direction from which we had fled when the camp was burned. There were holes in the grass all around us where soldiers and servitors had dug to find more of the squatter supply caches. They had found a handful containing spare bicycle parts, clothing, and polymer plates but none containing food.

We walked until we could barely hear the sound of the cargo jeeps rumbling in the distance. Oddly, the trees behind us were summer-green while the trees ahead seemed to be turning the colors of autumn. In the distance we heard the songs of meadowlarks, bobolinks, and passenger pigeons.

The landscape was like a nature painting from Old Earth. But as we walked, there were constant reminders that nothing here was truly natural. Here, a rounded stony outcropping just happened to form seats like a bench with backrests and lumbar support. There, a large boulder with a hollow opening like a bread oven. Next to it grew a stand of small plants—« milkweed »—whose fluffy white seedpods would make perfect tinder for starting a fire.

« It's nature but better. »

We found a place to rest in the thick, tall grass beneath an oak tree. It was the middle of the day, but we needed the relief that the Souven could offer.

We strapped it onto our head and slept for hours while the Souven flooded us with memories.

The machine was working so hard that soon it grew warm and sweat dripped from our head. The Souven was desperate to give us anything that might be useful. We remembered plants, edible and poisonous, from a dozen different biomes. We remembered the history of the Iter. We remembered working at a maritime loading dock, at a truck depot, in a spaceport. We remembered a dozen different evacuations, people fleeing a half-dozen worlds and habs.

It was so overwhelming that we lay there as if in a fever dream, unaware of our physical surroundings. Until the young woman shook us awake.

We pulled the goggles from our face.

"What are you doing here, Char?" we asked, disbelieving.

"I'm rescuing you," she said. "Come with me, quick and quiet."

We scanned around us quickly, but the area was still and there was no one else from REPO in sight. "Where are all the others?"

"A short way ahead," Char answered. "The Grasslanders baited them, and . . ." she looked embarrassed as she finished, "they kept moving without you."

« They left you behind. »

We hadn't told anyone where we had gone. They must not have seen us in the tall grass.

"Let's go," Char said, "before they come back."

We felt dizzy, still feverish from the Souven dreams. In the dream, we had been about to learn something. Or say something. Lethologica.

"What do you know about your ancestors?" we asked. "The Iter?"

She cocked her head, confused. "That was a long time ago. No one remembers much."

« The privilege of forgetting! »

"We remember something," we said. "They were radicals. Didn't believe in family wealth, opposed to inheritance. Owned things in common. They lived in peace until the People arrived and invaded their asteroid."

« They lived in peace, like us, until the People came. »

"What's an asteroid?" Char asked.

"A big rock in space that they had hollowed out to live in," we answered. "Like this, but cruder. When the People arrived, the Iter put up a resistance. But the Lord Commandant boxed some of the leaders, like they did your Uncle Tycho, and 'hired' the rest to build a pocket universe."

« Their asteroid became the bottleneck station. »

"After the pocket universe was stabilized, the Iter rebelled. Everyone there—thousands of people—evacuated into the injector. Into Germinal."

We expected Char to seem shocked at this revelation of her people's ancient past. But she didn't appear to care at all.

"We've got to go," she said.

"They were supposed to build a park here," we said. "They were supposed to make something for the rich to enjoy. But instead, they made something that reflected their values, didn't they? They tweaked the rules of the universe, so it matched their politics just a little bit more."

"Let's talk about this in a safe place," Char replied, shifting uneasily.

"But what would we do?" we asked. "If we came with you, what would we do all day?"

« To live is to serve. »

"Do as *you* please," Char enthused. "Try all the foods that land and sea have to share. Meet each culture and learn their languages. Watch birds. Make art and sing songs. Fix bikes or build wagons. Learn herbs to heal the ailing. Give thanks for every sunset with different friends. Walk the high forest walk, sail the ocean, or go to the desert to invent new communities. Teach children and tell stories."

« Yes! Tell them our stories. »

« Who could live such a selfish life as to do what *they* pleased? »

The thought of being so unmoored was terrifying, but something else nagged at us.

"Where do babies come from?" we asked.

Char nearly did a double take but acquiesced. "They come from the Spring People," she answered.

"No, I mean, how do they physically get made?"

"They're made in the flamewall," she said as if it were obvious, "when an old person on the other side is ready for their next life."

"But how does an old body get turned into a new one?" we asked, frustrated.

"How does an old palm tree get turned into a coconut?" she replied, as if that made everything clear.

"But what does that have to do with sex?" we asked, blushing slightly.

"Nothing!" she said, surprised at the abrupt change in topic, almost offended. "Except that you *choose* who you want to have sex with, and you *choose* who you build a cradle with, and sometimes those are the same people."

"We don't have flamewalls in the universe outside," we said. "So, when people want to make a baby, they usually make one by having sex."

For a second, she half-smiled, as if we'd made a joke. Then she appeared confused, then concerned when she realized we were serious. A moment later, she tried very hard to conceal her feeling of wide-open disgust until, finally, a look of realization.

"Ohh," she said, "like *animals*!"

"No!" we said reflexively, our turn now to feel affronted. Then, "Well, sort of like animals. But if you say that, it will offend people."

"Because they want to be animals," she said, processing, "but don't want to be *called* animals."

"They don't want to *be* animals!" we explained, exasperated. "It's just nature. It has nothing to do with *being* animals."

"But is this why the Conquis wants to hurt us?" she asked.

"The People have a very specific idea of what it means to be human," we said. "For them, that means you look a certain way, and your body works a certain way—that having sex and making babies are two parts of the same thing, for example."

"It's much better if they are separate," she said.

"No doubt," we agreed. "But they see your people as too different, and so the Conquis wants to hurt you."

"Being different can be good."

"You don't have to convince us!" we said. "But you must not tell the Conquis that we told you this."

She spent a moment turning these nested deceptions over in her mind. "How can we change his mind if we can't talk about it?"

"You can't," we said. "Absolutely nothing you say will change his mind. Ever." She frowned at this, so we added, "Not everyone is good, Char."

"But not everyone is bad, Graft!" she shot back.

A strange woman splattered with mud appeared from within the tall grass, then. We should have been surprised. But when everything is shocking, nothing is.

The woman whispered to Char in a voice like a breeze through green reeds. Then Char said to us, "Someone is coming back. We've got to run."

« Go with her. »

"We can't," we replied. "We need to stay with the Conquis. To keep him calm. If he gets upset, he could do something very bad."

"Listen—" Char began.

"Stop trying to convince people!" we said angrily. "You can't always fucking convince people!"

Char appeared startled, then hurt. The mud-spattered woman

gently grabbed her by the arm, and they fled almost silently toward the east, vanishing into the tall prairie grass.

We rubbed our face. There was still sleep in our eyes. Dried sweat encrusted the stubble on the sides of our head, and our maroon tunic was growing stained with grime. We yearned to find one of the little creeks, take off all our clothes, and bathe.

But before we could give into that urge, two soldiers arrived.

"The Conquis has been searching for you," one of them said.

« See! He does care. »

"A group of squatters has been captured," the soldier continued. "And the interrogation is about to begin."

Chapter 6

Decision

Char of the Ami

The rendezvous for the emergency meeting was in a thorny grove not far from the Amber Moon. When Boudica and I arrived, her son Aden was already waiting with Gus and Servitor Keegan and some bad news: a family of Grasslanders had been captured by the interlopers.

Boudica dropped me off and then sped away on a tandem bicycle with her son to see what could be done. I had nothing to do but wait for the arrival of my grandmother and the other delegates. I thought about brewing some friendship tea to calm my nerves, but I felt too anxious to do even that. So, I sat next to a clump of flowering bramble and vigilantly scanned our surroundings as Gus and Keegan dug into the ample supply of food the Forest People had sent with us.

Gus was also surveying our surroundings but for completely different reasons. "My goodness!" Gus exclaimed, still chewing. "There are avocados and apples growing from different branches of that same tree! The biochemistry boggles the mind."

"It's a buffet tree," I replied without turning to look, keeping watch on the paths nearby for the arrival of my grandmother and the rest of the delegation. "It's flame grafted."

"How did you do it?" Gus asked. "How did you create a stable ecology of this size?"

"I didn't create it," I replied.

"But your *ancestors* created it," he insisted. "Do you know how hard it is to balance an ecosystem in an enclosed space like this? Where I'm from, self-contained habs have separate algae facilities for oxygen generation, hydroponics, and so on. Any landscape more complicated than a lawn risks being overrun by pathogenic fungus. They have to burn out the microbiomes every few years and start again."

"I see," I answered, not really listening to the string of meaningless words.

"But *your* people figured that out! The flamewall offers continuous correction and adjustment!" he declared effusively. "This could be a Daisyworld! Tell me, does the balance of the biomes change over time to respond to climate shifts? Does the ratio of forest to grassland change over time?"

"The Grasslanders always want to graze more bison," I said. "The Forest People want to plant more trees. In the end, it all balances out."

"Amazing," he said. "Could the ecological balance of this universe be tied to the cultural behaviors of competing groups? For example, as the forest grows, it will sequester more of the carbon from the atmosphere, which would cause global cooling, yes? A cooler world means less evaporation from the seas, which means dryer weather. That would favor the spread of C4 grasses, bringing the world back into balance—are the grasses here C4? I would presume so. Oh, but how does the shifting size of each biome affect hunger and demographics?"

He was much chattier than the other interlopers I had met. Perhaps he dealt with stress by talking. "People move between different cultures as they wish," I said. "Teenagers and adults may choose to live in a different culture than the one in which they were raised."

"Of *course*!" he gushed. "Permeability of social groups would solve issues of local overpopulation! And it would be in keeping with your ancestors' opposition to rigid social strata." Then he gasped. My heart began to thump, and I spun to look in his direction to see if interlopers had snuck up on us. But Gus was simply staring into the sky, wide-eyed as if he had just realized something monumental.

"The flamewalls!" He spoke so quickly that I could barely understand him through his accent. "They don't only serve an *ecological* function. They have an economic and political dimension to prevent the uneven accumulation of wealth! The universe itself represents a shared *commons* in which private property is intrinsically limited to what you can carry!"

"Obviously," I said. "What we can't carry belongs to all of us. How could you own something you can't even move?"

"But no! No!" he said. "It's only obvious to you because you were raised in this context! To people from another culture, it would seem natural that the rich should continue to accumulate ever-more wealth and the poor should serve them unquestioningly." Then he glanced over to the servitor seated on the ground beside him. "Oh. Sorry, Keegan."

"Life is toil," the servitor replied, then giggled. I interrupted my watch of our surroundings to look at them both. Something odd was going on.

"I wonder," the Scitech said, "if the work of the Forest People constitutes a kind of loophole in the intent of the creators. They're able to accumulate physical wealth and infrastructure comprised of the bodies of the trees. Admittedly, their work is truly impressive—an architectural marvel!

"Speaking of which, I absolutely adore the decision to set gravity at seventy percent of Old Earth normal. It's so easy on the body," Gus continued, standing up, stretching out his legs then reaching his arms up above his head in a slight bend toward the sky. "But the sun is a bit too bright, if you ask me. More than is required for photosynthesis."

I stood and reached up to touch his shoulder. As he turned to gaze down at me, I saw his pupils were fully dilated, his eyelids drooping gently in his face. "Oh, thank you," he said, smiling, leaning into my hand on his shoulder. "That feels nice."

A glance at Keegan showed that his pupils, too, were wide. Crumpled on the ground around them were half a dozen empty leaf wrappers. I lifted one, and it smelled of bitter licorice.

"How many of these did you eat?" I asked.

"Oh, I'd say we've each had at least four," he said. "We were so hungry. And after you get past the bitter sauce, the fruit is delicious. What is it, an apple turnover?"

They'd eaten *four each.* Friendship wraps were meant to be shared, torn in half at diplomatic events so that two people with differing perspectives could share the same food. The intent was never for anyone to eat more than one in a day.

"It's a friendship wrap," I told him. "The bitter sauce represents difficult truth. And it keeps children from eating it by accident. The fruit inside is a . . . grown-up food."

His eyes went even wider then. Gus gaped at me for a moment, then studied his hands intently as if seeing them for the first time.

"It's psychoactive!" he realized. "A plant meant to resolve conflict and promote trust. Perhaps an endocannabinoid combined with a mild amphetamine or an agonist of oxytocin. It makes perfect sense that pharmacological needs would have botanical solutions in this world!"

"It's an empathogen, not an amphetamine. And you're going to need to drink a lot of water," I said, worried about the excessive dose. Fortunately, friendship wraps were fairly mild—unlike milkroot's powerful analgesics, which could make people fall asleep or even stop breathing if eaten in excess. "Don't eat any more of those." I paused, embarrassed at the cross-cultural faux pas. "I'm sorry for the miscommunication."

"No need to apologize!" Gus answered. "I'm having a great time."

It was then that the servitor spoke up. "Why aren't you guarding us?" he asked.

"You aren't our prisoner," I said. "You're our guest."

"But what if I'm a spy, gathering information?" he said. "What if as soon as I know where your people are hiding, I run back and report to the Conquis?"

"Oh my stars!" I gasped. "Is that what you're doing?"

"Of course not!" Keegan said. "I hate that fucker. But I *could* be, and you're just trusting me."

"But you're *not* spying on us," I clarified.

The servitor sighed in overt frustration. "I'm not spying on you," he said. "But if you want to beat those guys, you'll have to be a lot more suspicious of people!"

"We like to assume the best of people," I said.

"Yeah," the servitor frowned. "That's what I'm afraid of."

I felt profound relief when I saw my grandmother walking down the path in her red conciliator's scarf. I ran to her, and we hugged for a very long time.

She was followed closely by Ignatius, of Tapestry, and Alex Tern, of the Ternfolk.

"Are you okay?" she whispered into my hair.

"For now," I whispered back. "But where are the Forest People?"

"They aren't coming," she answered as she released me. "They have to hold some funerals." Funerals for unexpected deaths were a big deal for the Forest People—everyone stopped what they were doing to escort the bodies to the flamewall. It was much more formal than the Ami approach. "Where are the Grasslanders?" my grandmother asked.

"They went to try to help one of their families," I said. But before I could explain, we heard the sounds of someone approaching.

We turned to see Grasslander Aden, walking his tandem bicycle up to the path. He was alone, his mother nowhere to be seen. Even from a distance, we could see that his dirt-smeared face was tracked with tears.

Servitor Graft

The Conquis was in the midst of an interrogation when we returned. The soldiers had captured a woman with two children who had been hiding in tall grass to the east. They had also shot and killed another woman who had arrived then and tried to free them. And a different fire team had shot dead several more people in the forest, squatters who had tried to flee from the soldiers.

« They are monsters. »

It was true. And the Conquis was one, too. But for now, he was out of sight, questioning a prisoner inside one of the pop-up tents that the servitors would erect and take down each time we stopped in a grove of trees.

Our time with the Souven had finally given us a sense of greater understanding of the world we found ourself in. And of the people who built it, and why.

« They were not so different from us. »

And crucially—as we heard our stomach growl—we also remembered something about the plants around us. They were covered with food.

At one of the trees nearby, we found that each branch contained, oddly, a completely different fruit. We had never seen such things in person, but our ancestors recognized them: apples, pears, plums, apricots, all of them approaching ripeness.

One of the soldiers walked up and saw me observing the fruit tree.

"Is it food?" he asked. Our stomach growled in response.

« Don't tell him. »

"It's fruit," we answered, hesitantly.

"Like in a pie?" he said. "Fruit pie," made with flavored glucose, was one of the Meals-Ready-to-Eat most popular among the soldiers.

« Don't collaborate! »

Our answer caught in our throat. "They're poisonous," we lied, finally. "We can't eat them."

The soldier appeared equally disappointed and relieved. He had lived his entire life in a hab. The idea of eating fruit off a tree was about as appealing to him as eating live insects or raw meat.

"This world is hell," he said, shaking his head. "Everything here wants to kill us." He walked off.

« We are surrounded by plenty. »

Our stomach growled again, insistent, and we felt desperate to grab a plum from the tree and devour it, to let its juices drip onto our tunic the way our ancestors had.

Instead, we went to the temporary command tent. Two cots had been set up, though we wouldn't be staying in this spot long enough to use them. We had almost reached the site of the crash-landed drop-pod, and we expected the Conquis would want to proceed quickly once the interrogation was finished.

A short time later, the Conquis arrived, looking pale, and sat quietly on his cot. We slipped the Souven from inside our tunic and tucked it under our pillow. Then we busied ourself washing a pair of the Conquis's socks in a small basin, our back to the man. We rubbed the spot on our left thumb where we'd once had a scar. When he finally spoke, it was so softly that we could barely hear.

"Did you know?" he said, his voice like the hiss of a viper.

We froze in place.

"Did you know?" the Conquis asked again, quietly and dangerously.

We spoke without turning to face him, "Know what, Conquis?"

We heard the cot creak behind us as he shifted his weight. "What are you hiding from me?"

« Everything that matters. »

"Nothing, Conquis."

"Did you interrupt her on purpose?" he asked. "The girl, on

the first day. She was going to say something about the flamewall, to tell us the truth, but you interrupted. Did you know?"

We continued washing the socks, sinking our gaze into the basin of soapy water. "We know nothing about this world," we answered.

"Lies!" he hissed through his teeth. "You knew about the time slippage. You knew which dialect to use with them. How did you know that?"

"The scientists learned about the time slippage," we said, letting the socks drop into the washbasin. We turned toward him, still looking down. "The ancestors told us about the dialect."

"The ancestors," he mused, "in your dream machine." He reached over to our bed in the corner of the little tent we shared and pulled the Souven out from its place under our pillow. We stiffened silently, involuntarily, as we watched.

The Conquis turned it over skeptically, flipping it back and forth, as if the machine that contained the whole of our ancestral memories were a stale piece of bread he was checking for mold.

"How odd that this is the only databank that arrived unscathed," he said. "Why do you think that is?"

The ancestors were silent, as if holding their collective breath.

"We don't know, Conquis. The scientists are working to—"

"Do you sympathize with them, Graft?" he interrupted. "A bunch of oddballs with weird cultural traditions, talking funny and shut up in their own strange world. Does that seem *familiar* to you, Graft? Do you *identify* with that?"

"Not at all, my conqueror," we replied. "We are nothing like them."

"Do you think we should treat them gently?" he coaxed. "Give them a slap on the wrist? Maybe even let them stay in some corner of the world they stole?"

« Be careful. »

"Not at all, Conquis," we answered, keeping our eyes still carefully lowered. "They have committed crimes against the People."

We stared at the ground for a long time, waiting for the Conquis to speak. A dark beetle made its way through the trampled grass at our feet. The Souven was still in the clenched hand of the Conquis. We saw him squeeze it, hard.

"Last time, Graft," he said. "Did. You. Know."

"Know what, Conquis?" we whispered, seeing the irreplaceable Souven held in his meaty fist.

He stood abruptly, so that his face was only inches from ours in the closeness of the tent. His words were choked, almost like a shout, as he rasped angrily, "They don't have babies! They don't give birth!"

We looked up in shock. Shocked that he had discovered this so quickly.

"Ex-*actly!*" he spat. We flinched at the spray of saliva. But he threw the Souven down onto his cot and began to pace the confines of the tent.

"The boy-hostage admitted everything," the Conquis said quietly, rubbing the back of his neck and tugging on the key-necklace there. "He said it without an ounce of shame. He told us how they make cradles out of sticks and stones, how their elderly willingly burn themselves alive, how the flamewall takes some piece of them, and . . . and remakes them as a baby!"

We were not sure what parts of this to believe. Had the prisoner spun a ridiculous tale to deceive his captors? Had the Conquis finally snapped?

"They are fucking *reincarnated*, Graft!" he said, his voice still lowered as though afraid someone might overhear the disgusting details. "Without their memories, perhaps. But with something. With the same eyes! Copies of copies, forever. The hostage told us this as if it were . . . *beautiful*!"

He sat back down on his cot—nearly crushing the Souven—and covered his face with his hands, in true distress.

We waited for the insight of the ancestors, but nothing came. They were as speechless as we were at the specifics.

"Adults just *find* the babies in the cradles they make," he said through his fingers. "The fire leaves the babies there, asleep, covered in a *paste* that makes the adults lactate. Woman or man! That's how they become parents and breastfeed the little monsters!"

He rubbed his eyes, lowered his hands, and leaned forward, resting his elbows on his knees.

"This is the worst case of human degeneracy we've ever come across," he sighed. "Worse than the wisp-men of Gliese, even. These squatters are beyond imagination. I thought we could salvage the children, at least. But this . . ." he trailed off.

« Under the red light of Gliese 581, a twitching tumbleweed screams during its incineration. »

« This will change things. » The ancestors were right. It was an inflection point in how the Conquis would treat the people here. He saw them as more than mere squatters now. As something worse, something inhuman. His goal and his duty would not be to prosecute them now but to eradicate them.

After a few moments the Conquis sat up, straighter, as if remembering something. "We must get to the other beacon and set up the landing zone," he said. "The Commandant will know what to do."

Char of the Ami

When the meeting delegates finally assembled, there were representatives from each major group—save the Forest People—sitting in a circle on inflatable Ami-style cushions that had been pulled from a nearby cache. Aden, still openly weeping over the death of his mother in a skirmish with the interlopers, insisted on coming. But he sat slumped against Alex, the Ternfolk rep, who was comforting him, gently stroking his hair.

The interlopers were represented by Gus and Keegan, still smiling and relaxed as if everything were good in the universe.

Three Ami were present. Myself, as a witness. Ignatius, no doubt present to assert the Tapestry position. And my grandmother, serving as chair and ad hoc conciliator.

"Where is the Forest speaker?" asked Alex Tern. His forehead was painted black and his lips orange. This was the usual Ternfolk attire, in homage to the bird after which they took their name. For this official occasion, Alex had even glued small white feathers behind his ears.

"The Forest People have declined to send a delegate," my grandmother said. "They have funerals to attend to and believe that a meeting should wait until after the dead have been mourned and given to the flamewall."

"It must be nice," said Grasslander Aden, his dusty face tracked with tears, "to hide in the trees when all of Germinal is in danger."

"A proposal has been made," my grandmother said, "that all Habitants should band together and attack the interlopers. I have never chaired a meeting with such a grim premise."

"It's far too early to discuss violence," Ignatius said. Despite the warm weather and the dense brush and thorns around us, he wore his full ceremonial garb: a bison-fur hat from the Grasslanders, a fish-scale necklace from the Ternfolk, bark bracelets from the Forest People, desert sandals and, of course, the multicolored, striped poncho that gave his sect their name. Clearly, asserting his expertise at the meeting of delegates was worth the risk of tearing his tapestry on a thornbush. He added, "We haven't even had a discussion with the interloper leaders. That must be our first step."

"You did not see their deeds," the Grasslander replied. "The bison they maimed. The people they killed."

"I'm sorry for your losses in the skirmish," Ignatius replied. "But a battle takes two sides. Is it not that—"

"Argument," my grandmother interrupted, "comes second. Facts come first. Now I will hear facts." She turned to me, and I spoke, outlining the bare bones of what I had done and witnessed since the taboo message from the Spring People had arrived, what had happened to Tycho, my discussions with Graft, and how I had come to meet Doctor Gustafsen and Servitor Keegan.

When I had finished, the group was quiet, digesting the many unsettling details I had shared. My grandmother seemed pensive, almost lost in thought—thinking, no doubt, of the torment of her son Tycho—until I coughed.

"Thank you, Char," she said. "Servitor Keegan and Doctor Gustafsen, can you verify for the others what Char has told us?"

"Absolutely," Gus replied, his face expressive. "The Conquis is a monster. He and the Commandant will do *whatever they can* to take back this universe. You've got to stop them by any means necessary or you're done for." His pupils were still dilated.

It was unsettling to see someone who had eaten friendship wraps say such terrible things.

"Servitor Keegan?" my grandmother prompted.

I could see the whites of his eyes from across the circle, anxious; he wasn't used to being called on in this way. "Please call me Keegan," he said. "I'm not a servitor anymore." Grandmother nodded and waited for him to continue. But he said nothing more.

Ignatius spoke into the silence. "I think I speak for everyone when I say that more violence is not the solution," he declared. "No one wants another Blue Moon Brawl. Did these strangers do things that we find unacceptable? Absolutely. Is their behavior odd? Of course! But because they do not know our ways. The Grasslander raids, I am sorry to say, have probably made things worse. We need to *talk* to these strangers."

"Tycho tried to talk to them," I reminded him.

"Tycho went off on his own," Ignatius replied. "Without a conciliator, without a speaker from Tapestry. He should have called a meeting with us instead of rushing in."

"He was trying to help me," I said.

"An admirable act," he said. "But when we charge in without thinking, we make disagreements worse! We must try a nonviolent resolution before doing anything hasty. I propose a formal meeting with the visitors. A peace offering."

"You don't know what they are like," I said. "You didn't see them firsthand, like I did."

"With respect, young woman," he chided, "you are too personally involved in this dispute to be objective about it."

"It's not a dispute, it's an invasion!" I snapped back. Ignatius nodded sympathetically—almost smugly—as if my sharp tone had validated his point. My grandmother's face was blank. Her role as conciliator required neutrality in this moment.

"She's right," Gus said, and Aden, who had stopped crying, murmured his agreement. "Look, you don't get it, because you lack cultural context," said Gus. "But these people really want to control everything. And they don't think you have any right to be here. You've got to act fast."

Ignatius squinted at Gus, then examined him up and down ostentatiously. "Pardon me, sir, but are you intoxicated?"

The Scitech smiled happily, and I blushed. "There was a mix-up," I said, "with the refreshments."

Ignatius frowned. "I do not think we can accept advice—or so-called facts—from people in such a state," he said.

"Gus may be a lightweight," Aden said, "but he's right. The interlopers have been relentless. If we are going to stop them, we should do it now."

"We should converse with them," Ignatius repeated. "Call for a meeting."

"You're not *listening* to us," I said. "We have to act quickly."

He raised one eyebrow and adjusted his ceremonial garment, straightening the hem, as if to say, *Look at all these stripes I got for listening*. Then he added, "What would your parents think of this, this . . . bloodthirst?"

I scowled, and the Grasslander spoke up, "You don't understand because no Ami died at their hands," Aden said. "Grasslanders died. Forest People died. You're up here on a comfortable cushion."

Ignatius sighed. "We should all try to bring peace. I'm sad for the Grasslanders and for the Forest People. But if we lash out over someone else's grievance, we will always be trapped in cycles of escalating violence."

"They want to destroy us," I said.

"You don't know that," Ignatius said. "*We* don't *know* what they want until we talk to them ourselves."

Gus spoke. "Maybe I'm missing something because of the dialectical differences," he said, "but is it just me or is this guy full of shit?"

Ignatius looked affronted. "How dare you?"

"You should go right now," Gus said. "If you're so sure, walk down there yourself. You'll end up in a fucking box inside of ten minutes."

There was a charged silence as everyone watched Ignatius. "It would be a stronger showing," he demurred, "if we all sent a delegation together. But, if necessary, I will go my own way."

....

Tapestry adherents earned their stripes by spending years with each culture, wandering Germinal from pole to pole learning the customs of each people. Learning their cuisines, their histories, their dialects, and their ways of making decisions.

Decision-making among the Forest People was consensus-based to a fault. The mangrove circuit had famously spent seventeen years arguing whether to build a fish weir on a particular stream. One of the participants in the discussion had camped next to the stream for two entire laps—spring, summer, and fall, twice over—counting every single fish that swam up and down the stream, hoping to bolster their case. In the end, natural erosion had solved the disagreement when shifting sediment pushed the stream into the path of another river, rendering the argument moot.

The Forest People, with their love of ecological infrastructure, frequently had such disputes. The Ternfolk were the opposite. If two boats were moored at the same dock and an argument arose that couldn't be resolved over the course of a single shared meal, they would untie their sailboats and head in opposite directions. Of course, the next time they found themselves fishing the same shoal they would be perfectly friendly, as if they had never quarreled. What reason had they to hold a grudge?

The desert polities exhibited both extremes. Each one of their communities was made up of people who had decided to try an entirely different way of life from what existing cultures could offer. They had banded together—perhaps at a Convergence—to try some entirely new approach to decision-making or economics or family relationships. They would argue politics from dawn until dusk and then again all through the night. And though they had split off from the communities of their childhood, most of them hoped to one day bring their social innovations back to the broader world.

The Ami fell somewhere in the middle of these different approaches. We had plenty of conciliators. And a sizable group of Tapestry adherents who would talk anything through ad nauseam. Plenty of differences had been solved around a campfire late into the night, with the gentle guidance of a facilitator.

But plenty of arguments had *worsened* the same way, too, of course. There was lots of land, and none of it belonged to any one person. So, if arguments flared, opposing parties would just travel separately for a while until tempers cooled and they came to an agreement. Or not. The sun would rise and set either way.

We Ami called this "going your own way." Consensus was nice, but if we couldn't reach it, everyone would go their own way for a while. It was one of our central political principles going back centuries. And it almost always worked out.

Until today.

The sprawling, frustrating discussion about the interlopers had not resulted in any consensus on how to respond. So, Ignatius had decided to go his own way. Which in this case, meant that he planned to walk over to the Amber Moon alone and try to broker a peace treaty with the interlopers.

"You can't let him do that," Gus told me after the meeting had adjourned for dinner." His radical honesty won't work with the Conquis or the Commandant. They'll eat him alive."

"What?!" I exclaimed, astonished by the ceaseless parade of depravity.

Gus and Keegan exchanged glances. "Not literally," Gus clarified. "I mean, the Conquis will take advantage of his naivety."

I sighed, only slightly relieved. "I can't stop him from going down there tomorrow. It's every Ami's right to roam and talk to whoever wishes to talk to them."

"Listen, Gus is correct," said Keegan. "If Ignatius talks to the Conquis, he will give away every tactical advantage you have. And if the Commandant finds out about how you, uh, reproduce, he'll kill every one of you."

I stared at him a few moments. "And that's *not* a metaphor," he said.

"Let's be clear," Gus said, "I'd prefer if you just locked Ignatius in a wagon for a few days—"

"He's joking," added Keegan.

"I'm not," continued Gus, "but if you can't stop him from going, you need to send people who can manage the conversation. Steer it away from dangerous areas. And keep Ignatius from giving up useful information."

"Until what?" I asked.

"Maybe the Forest People will come!" Keegan said, hopefully. I frowned, doubtful.

"Let us sleep on it," Gus said. "We'll talk it through."

"Ok," I agreed, "but I can't promise much."

Keegan shrugged. "Well," he said, "neither can we."

....

For dinner that night we joined up with the rest of the Ami who were camped not far away. It was too dangerous to start a campfire, so we ate a simple, cold dinner of fruit and smoked salmon.

Gus was coming down from his friendship-wrap high. But he was still gregarious and seized the opportunity to converse with the Ami about his area of interest.

"I study universes, you see," Gus told a circle of Ami, as he ate a wedge of orange.

"He is one of the most learned men I've ever met," Keegan agreed. And then added, in case it wasn't clear, "He's very smart."

"I'd like to ask you some questions," Gus began, "about your world, about Germinal. First of all," he said, "what is *outside* of it?"

The Ami looked at one another. "The world is *inside*," my cousin Theo said. "When the world was inside-out, it was broken. That's why we came here."

The scientist tried again. "What I mean is, we can see the sphere that makes up the world." He picked up an empty wicker fruit basket and held it up on his fingertips. It seemed to glow in the sideways light of the setting sun. "The world is a sphere, and the inside of the basket is like the ground we are sitting on. There is air around the basket. But what is around the universe? What is underneath the ground we are sitting on?"

"Not air," came the immediate response from Aunt Scarlet. "If there were empty air under the ground, the ground would crumble into it!" The Ami chuckled at the scientist's ignorance, as if to say, *If this is the smartest person the interlopers had, no wonder those people were in so much trouble.*

"Certainly," the scientist replied. "So, what *is* holding up the ground? What if we dug far down into the ground?"

The Ami stopped chuckling. Some glanced toward Grandmother.

Grandmother frowned and said, "That would be dangerous."

"Why?" he demanded. "What would I find if I dug a very deep hole?"

She fixed him with a gaze that was nearly a glare. "You would find a fool at the bottom of a hole." Then she got up and walked away.

That signaled to the other Ami that the group conversation had ended, and a dozen side-conversations began immediately. The sky had grown dark and quiet, as the first stars emerged from the east.

Gus turned to me, "Did I say something wrong?"

"We live in a generous world," I told him. "A world that gives freely. But if you try to take something the world doesn't want to give, bad things can happen."

He paused, considering. "Someone tried that experiment," he said, a shadow crossing his face in the fading red sunlight. Perhaps he wasn't as naive as he seemed.

"When my grandmother was a child," I confirmed. "It went very badly."

I went in search of my grandmother, stepping carefully between dark tents and wagons. I found her where I expected, in the thick, dry grass in front of Cousin Theo's tent. She was holding the sleeping purple-eyed baby, Quang Duc.

"Can I make you some tea, Grandmother?" I asked.

She was gazing softly at the child and didn't seem to hear my words. "We'll break camp at dawn," she told me. "Send anyone who can't fight further west, near the sea. They can paddle to the safety of the polar islands if they have to. You'll guide the children."

"No!" I said, more stridently than I meant to. "When the bicycle archers arrive, I'm going back with them to get Uncle Tycho." The baby fussed slightly in its sleep, and she held it closer.

"You are grown, and it's your decision," she said. "You can choose to do dangerous things. But don't do this out of guilt. What happened to Tycho wasn't your fault."

"I don't feel guilty!" I lied, hot tears in my eyes. "I feel angry!"

She didn't say anything, just shifted the child slightly toward her right arm, so that she could beckon me toward her. I didn't hesitate and crawled onto the grass next to her and into her arms. As stars spread across the sky, my tears spilled over onto my grandmother's soft red scarf.

....

I couldn't fall asleep. Some time later, I got up, left my grandmother and Quang Duc snoring, and walked to stretch my legs. Not far away I came across Gus and Keegan. Gus had raised his shirt and Keegan was inspecting his bare back.

"What's going on?" I asked.

"Just checking for ticks," said Keegan.

"What's a tick?"

Gus made an odd face. "Eight-legged arthropod," he said. "Lives in the grass? Crawls up under your clothes when you aren't paying attention and sucks your blood?"

"Oh no!" I said, horrified. "I've never heard of that."

Keegan sighed. "Next you'll tell us that you don't have any mosquitoes."

I shook my head. "I don't think so."

"It truly is a utopia!" Gus said, shaking his head and laughing. I couldn't tell if he was joking or not.

"It's not a utopia," I replied. "We have lots of annoying people."

"Hmmm," Keegan considered. "Perhaps we know that we are living in utopia when our biggest problem is being annoyed by other people."

"On that topic," Gus said, "we've been talking with your Aunt Scarlet about how to handle the Conquis and this 'peace treaty' nonsense."

"I don't think you'll like it," Keegan said. "It's a huge risk. But we do have an idea."

Chapter 7
Peace and War

Servitor Graft

The beacon began to ring out just after sunrise, a sequence of chimes in perpetual crescendo. It was an alert of an incoming vessel we could not yet see. The lieutenant grabbed the beacon and placed it out in the open space on top of the Amber Moon to guide the distant craft.

The Conquis shouted for everyone to muster, and muster they did, hurling their half-eaten paper bowls of porridge into a pile and rushing to the edge of the landing zone. The Conquis, with gestures and staccato grunts, straightened their ragged lines into columns—soldiers in the middle, scientists on the right, and servitors left and to the back.

« Like a little boy trying to impress a distant father. »

Once they were all in strict formation, there was just enough time left for us to straighten the Conquis's coat, slick down a stray wisp of hair, and blot a spot of blood from his lapel.

We caught our first view of the Lord Commandant's majestic craft as it emerged slowly from a cumulus cloud far overhead. *The Preserver* was no overloaded military drop-pod, firing its engines desperately to keep from slamming into the ground. It was a gleaming chariot, twice as long as a drop-pod and a quarter of the weight, drifting gently down toward the beacon. Her sides were resplendent in gold-coated ceramic tiles. The Conquis, we saw, had tears in his eyes at the wonder of it.

« It's a ship of brutal conquest », an ancestor reminded me, « no matter how shiny. »

The Commandant's craft slid down toward us, igniting her thrusters at only the last possible moment, alighting on the rocky mesa, showering us with whatever loose bits of grit and debris the servitors had been unable to sweep away overnight.

We blinked our eyes to clear the dust as the thrusters went silent. The Commandant's chariot was before us, a long golden craft balanced on legs like the stems of crystal wine glasses. Everything on the craft reflected or refracted the morning sunlight, to spectacular effect.

« And who labored to build this beautiful ship of death? »

The soldiers and scientists broke into applause at the sight of it. The servitors kept their heads bowed and their hands clasped.

The delay was just a bit longer than usual. We waited for the toxic gas from the thrusters to clear away and then the door of the ship—not a hatch but a wide entry panel—canted out and upward to create a sunshade. Stairs unfolded to the ground, stopping just above the surface of engine-charred rock. Then two of the white-clad honor guard emerged with a roll of gold-trimmed carpet the color of eggshell, which they deployed from the foot of the stairs so that it unrolled toward us.

The Conquis signaled the two surviving musicians of REPO—the bugle player and the drummer—who began their rendition of the Psalm of Triumph. The bugle player did a serviceable job, under the circumstances.

The first two honor guardsmen positioned themselves on either side of the stairs, at attention. The soldiers in the REPO contingent straightened.

We listened to the ascending melody of the Psalm of Triumph and waited.

And waited. The bugle player finished the final bars of the Psalm and then—after a moment of hesitation that put him out of sync with the drummer—began the Psalm again from the beginning.

Finally, gilded white boots appeared at the top of the stairs, as the Lord Commandant descended. He wore alabaster jodhpurs and a golden cuirass beneath a voluminous lavender-hued cloak. He strode down the carpet, an honor guardsman at each side. He was a mirror image of the Conquis, except that his clothes were bright and clean where the Conquis's were dingy and field worn. The Commandant's cuirass shone while the Conquis's was scuffed. Even the Commandant's high cheekbones seemed chiseled from white marble while the Conquis's scarred jowls were covered in stubble as we'd been continuously on the move.

The two men shook hands as the musicians finished their second rendition. "So, then," said the Lord Commandant, in his rich baritone, "how goes the war?"

The Commandant's expression was stern and friendly in equal measure. Surely the Commandant could answer his own question. REPO force had but a single drop-pod, sitting askew on the rock shelf nearby, propped on its broken leg. More than half the soldiers were missing, there were only a handful of tents and vehicles left, and VANGUARD was entirely gone.

Despite the obvious state of affairs, the Conquis put on a good show. "We have the enemy on the back foot, my lord. We have captured important prisoners and driven off squatters who had attempted an ambush."

"Good, good," the Commandant nodded.

"We have sustained some losses due to unexpected environmental factors."

"I see," the Commandant replied, still nodding.

"But with your leadership, we can complete the campaign in short order," the Conquis concluded.

"Yes, of course," the Commandant agreed. There was a brief pause.

« Military protocol requires the words "I relieve you of command, sir," followed by the corresponding reply "I stand relieved." »

The Conquis pressed on, mildly concerned. "I trust your injection was favorable, my lord, and the descent was in order?"

"Yes, quite," answered the Commandant.

The Conquis waited. Then he cleared his throat, and added, "My lord, do you have any questions before assuming command?"

"Of course, absolutely," the Commandant replied. His expression was oddly blank.

Both honor guardsmen stood at attention, face forward, but one was peeking at the Commandant out of the corner of his eyes.

The Conquis was unsure how to handle this divergence from

protocol. "My lord, I will answer any questions I can. What do you wish to know?"

Confusion passed briefly over the Commandant's features and then his face returned to a posture of stern conviviality. "So, then!" he said, brightly. "How goes the war?"

....

"Has he had a stroke?" the Conquis demanded.

The only doctor in REPO had been lost to the flames. The chief scientist along with a biologist who specialized in regenerative algae tanks had been forced to take up his duties

"We don't have the equipment to check properly," the biologist replied, "but he doesn't show any symptoms, such as one-sided weakness. Their descent wasn't even a high-g maneuver."

The Commandant had been brought to a tent that served both as medical bay and storage depot. He was seated on a bed made of crates and nodded vigorously along to the conversation.

"What can we do to restore his memory?" the Conquis asked.

The biologist sighed. "I have no idea. We would have to know if the problem is in the electrical layer of his brain." He stared at the Commandant as if he could peer through the man's skull to diagnose his defective brain. "Or if the neurons have actually been rewired."

"Of course. Quite," the Commandant said.

The chief scientist added, "It may have something to do with the information filtering Gustafsen spoke of. That when he was injected into this reality, the world itself stripped away vital military information."

The Conquis was unconvinced. "But he says only nonsense."

« He cannot remember anything else. Lethologica. »

We spoke up. "Conquis," we said, "perhaps the Commandant's mind was so absolutely full of vital military knowledge, the knowledge of how to rule, that once it was removed . . ."

"There was almost nothing left," inferred the biologist.

« He was an irredeemable shit », an ancestor agreed.

This raised the question of why the Conquis remembered so much. Though, on reflection, the Conquis had perhaps exercised more restraint than usual since we had arrived on Germinal. Was it that he had forgotten some of his habitual ruthlessness? Had some of his desire for atrocity been stripped out of him on arrival?

The Conquis paled, his skin even waxier than usual. "I will allocate any resources required to solve this."

"Absolutely," the Commandant agreed with gruff enthusiasm.

"I interned at a neurology rehab clinic in grad school," said the biologist, with growing passion for the problem. "Based on my time there, assuming we can get access to nootropic medications and a portable fMRI machine, I think we could develop a course of treatment in as little as six months."

There was a lengthy pause. "Dismissed," the Conquis uttered through clenched teeth. The two scientists left.

The Conquis and the Commandant stared at one another for a long time in silence. The Conquis rested a hand on the Commandant's shoulder.

« See », said an ancestor, « even he is capable of sympathy. »

The Conquis raised his other hand, grasped the lapel of the Commandant's lavender cloak, and pulled it snug against the old man's neck. Then, holding the lapel of the cloak with both hands, he began to squeeze. The Commandant's face turned red; his eyes appeared to pop.

We watched, frozen in horror and fascination. The honor guard was just outside. A shout would alert them and save the Commandant's life.

« Gyaku jūji-jime », remarked an ancestor coldly. « A traditional collar choke in Judo. »

The Commandant's confusion had turned to panic. He reached up clumsily to bat away the Conquis's hands, already losing consciousness.

« The Commandant destroyed our home. He deserves nothing better. »

« He ruined us! This mercy is too good for him! »

Before we could speak there was a shout from outside, "Squatters approaching the camp!"

The Conquis released his superior from his grip, and the old man slumped against the crates beside him, breathing heavily. The Conquis looked at us with surprise, as though he had forgotten we were there. Then he turned to leave the tent.

"Don't let the Commandant outside," he told the honor guard as he left. "He is disorientated. Keep him here and keep him safe."

Char of the Ami

I breathed deeply as we stepped out of the grove and onto the sandstone steps of the Amber Moon. It was a short climb to the flat mesa above, but it meant leaving the cover of the trees and tall grasses below. Once we reached the top of the large rocky plateau, the high open ground, no one could sneak up and save us at the eleventh hour—not the Forest People, not the Grasslanders, and not the Ternfolk.

Our "peace delegation" was a small, ragtag group. Waving a flag of harmony, Ignatius walked at the head of the group, with my grandmother and myself trailing behind. Gus and Keegan followed me, along with two Ami carrying full backpacks. Alex Tern brought up the very end of the line. Absent were the Grasslanders, who had formally declined to participate, and the Forest People, who were still occupied with funerals and group discussion.

The interloper sentries spotted us quickly on the flat, rocky plain and trained their weapons on us from a distance. We walked slowly so as not to alarm them. By the time we approached speaking distance, Conquis was waiting for us at the edge of their perimeter.

"Stop there," he said, when we were about twenty feet away. "You will enter our base only by invitation."

The word "base" was generous, especially in comparison to their original encampment. They had only four tents, a crooked silver airboat, and a long, golden ship that reminded me of a shark. Their clothing was filthy, their numbers noticeably reduced. I scanned for Graft and did not see him out in the open, but I caught a glimpse of a tall figure in maroon watching from behind the door of a tent, its flap barely parted.

"I am Ignatius," our Tapestry representative announced. "I am called 'He Who Listens Before Speaking.'" I suppressed the urge to roll my eyes.

"Sergeant-Conquistador First Class Mandrel Hannover," he replied, omitting his long string of titles, perhaps due to his obvious exhaustion. "I stand ready to accept your surrender."

"We are here to offer peace," Ignatius replied. To Conquis, I suspected, peace and surrender were much the same thing. "We have brought an offering of food to show our good will." The Ami with backpacks stepped forward and laid them on the ground. One of the interloper soldiers eyed the bags in obvious hunger.

"How can you speak of peace when you hold two of our own as prisoners?" Conquis asked, gesturing at Gus and Keegan. "Or have you come to return them?"

"We keep no prisoners," Ignatius replied. "We have fed these two and kept them safe."

"This is not going well," Gus whispered to me. "You should offer an exchange for your uncle."

My grandmother's thoughts were the same. "I am the Red Grandmother of the Westernmost Ami," she said, "and you are keeping my son Tycho and several other prisoners here against their will."

Grandma and Conquis stared at each other for several long breaths, each saying nothing. Conquis shifted and I wasn't sure if he was about to blink or pull his gun when Ignatius stepped forward.

"We all got off on the wrong foot," Ignatius said. "When you arrived, there were misunderstandings. When misunderstandings escalate, there can be violence. No one wants that."

Conquis tilted his head, listening like a curious dog. Watching, like a grassland archer judging the distance of her target. Then he broke into a broad smile, showing dark molars the color of carbon fiber.

"We really *did* get off on the wrong foot!" he agreed. "This world seemed so strange and confusing."

"It must be very different from your home universe," Ignatius empathized.

"*Very* different," Conquis said, his smile transitioning into puppy-dog eyes. "Our cosmos is a harsh place. Not like this. And so, when the fire arrived, we were confused and frightened."

"It can happen to the best of us," Ignatius acknowledged. "We are sorry for the loss of your people in the flamewall. We should have warned you about the special dangers here."

"We lashed out," Conquis admitted. "We lashed out in fear and anger. And we're real sorry about that."

"What the fuck is happening?" I whispered to Gus.

"The Conquis has your buddy's number," he replied in a hush.

"Our people are also afraid," Ignatius said. "Would you be willing to release the Habitants who are traveling with you, in order to relieve their worries?"

"Oh, of course," said the Conquis, turning to a nearby soldier. "Bring forward the woman and children."

There was a pause as three hostages—a women and two children—were brought from a nearby tent. Ignatius turned and caught my eye. *See how dialogue works?* his smug expression said.

"Oh, that's bad," Gus hissed beneath his breath. It didn't seem that way to me, but Gus clarified, "He doesn't think he needs hostages anymore."

The three Grasslanders looked dirty and worse for wear but not seriously hurt. The Ami who had put down their packs now moved to escort the hostages back the way we had come.

"A gesture of our good will!" Conquis announced grandly, smiling again so broadly I could see his back teeth. "I trust you'll do the same."

At a nod from my grandmother, Gus and Keegan stepped forward, each picking up one of the backpacks of food as they walked into the interloper camp. Neither of them looked back.

"We thank you," Ignatius said, his voice growing louder so everyone could hear. "This is a great step forward for all our people. A step toward peace."

"Let the Forefathers hear!" the Conquis exclaimed.

"A joyous day," Ignatius answered. "There remains still the issue of Tycho. I understand he is sealed in a container of some kind."

"It will take time to unbox him safely. We will begin at once," the Conquis promised. He did not glance at any of his men when he said this, nor did any of the soldiers move from where they stood. "Ignatius, may I ask a favor of you?"

"Of course, Conquistador Hannover," Ignatius intoned, as though the words were made of honey.

"We have an injured man," the Conquis said. "I understand that young Char here has some expertise in medicine. While her uncle is being decarcerated, perhaps she could examine our casualty?"

"Absolutely," said Ignatius, turning to me with a smile.

....

I entered the sick man's tent, but the first person I saw there was Graft. He glanced at me ever so briefly, his shadowed eyes a warning. Reflexively, I paused in the doorway, but Conquis pushed me the rest of the way in.

Inside was a man dressed in flowing white and gold with a purple cape, sitting on a bed of crates. "He has a problem with his memory," Conquis said.

I looked at the man in the golden cuirass, who was older than Tycho but younger than Grandmother. The old man scowled back at me. "Yes, yes," he said dismissively.

"Have you forgotten something?" I asked.

"Of course!" he spat, his voice derisive, his eyes empty.

"Can you tell me what?"

"Absolutely!" he said, shooting Conquis a dirty look. But he only scoffed quietly to himself and stared into the middle distance. I looked to Graft, who avoided my gaze.

I took a guess: "Have you forgotten . . . *everything*?"

"Yes, yes," said the man, with the bored tone of someone waiting to get to the end of a conversation.

"Do your people have treatments for memory problems?" Conquis asked. "Is this something that happens here?"

"Old people can be forgetful," I said, using truth to avoid the question. "We can find some medicine that helps with memory." That was also the truth, but there was no herb for complete amnesia. "But if someone has forgotten how to do everything . . ."

"Then it's time to send them into the flamewall," Conquis answered, "to be born again."

I held my breath. I couldn't look at him. I glanced again at Graft and unexpectedly met his gaze—the sight of him staring back at me was electric. The tent's door was so close. I turned to flee but felt a steel grip on my forearm.

It wasn't Conquis. It was the old man, his strong fingers digging into my muscle. "How goes the war?!" he demanded. But he didn't sound angry.

Conquis took hold of my wrist, lifted it, and began prying the man's hand off my arm, finger by finger, as the old man grunted in discomfort.

"Don't worry about him," Conquis told me. "He doesn't want you to go. He doesn't want to be left alone with me." It was true. The old man's eyes were wide with fear. Conquis finished removing the man's hand but kept his hold on my wrist. "No matter. We have other things to worry about."

He crouched down to stare directly into my eyes, without letting go of my wrist.

"I need you to act normal," he said. "For the next while, whatever happens, I need to you to act like everything is fine."

"Things are not fine," I sneered back.

"If you don't," he said, "I'm going to walk out there, and I'm going to shoot your grandmother in the heart." I gasped despite myself. "And then I'm going to shoot that loudmouthed idiot in the rainbow shirt and then that weird motherfucker with the orange lipstick. And I won't take them to the flamewall. I'm going to kill them all and throw them in the back of the jeep with your uncle."

My chest pounded like a drum, my hands clenched into fists, and the sound of blood rushed through my ears.

"They are never going to reincarnate," he said, "and they're never going to have a moment's rest because I'm going to drive them in circles around this world until their bodies rot while the dried husk of your uncle rattles around like a dead bug in that casket."

I lost all feeling in my body—I didn't even feel like I *had* a body. I was overtaken by an existential dread that went beyond fear, a horror beyond fight-or-flight. I had never imagined that anyone could even think of something so terrible, let alone threaten to do it to people I cared about.

"And that's why," the Conquis explained, with his broad smile, "for the next thirty minutes, you are going to act like everything is perfectly fine. No matter what happens."

Servitor Graft

The Conquis led Char out of the tent by the arm. We followed a moment later, nauseated by what we had just heard, struggling to drive it from our thoughts. The Conquis strode toward the center of camp, where his lieutenant stood.

The rest of the "peace delegation" was still at the edge of the camp. A man wearing a rainbow-colored poncho was speaking enthusiastically with the chief scientist while beside him an old woman with white hair stared daggers at the Conquis from a distance. Char didn't once return her gaze.

Nearby, some of the servitors had set up an improvised buffet table on the back of a jeep, laying out the food that the Ami had given as a peace offering. Soldiers were already devouring it, elbowing servitors and Scitechs aside to gorge on baked goods. Servitor Keegan had returned to camp and was helping to serve the food. We made eye contact for just an instant, but he looked away quickly.

« What is he hiding? »

"Bring me a beacon," the Conquis instructed his lieutenant. Char stood beside him, her arms crossed.

"Conquis," we said, "you must be hungry. Why not pause for breakfast?"

"Get me amphor," he replied dismissively.

We went to find the amphor case. By the time we returned to the center of camp, the lieutenant had fetched the beacon and was standing watch over Char, who had been made to sit on the sandstone ground. The Conquis, however, was absent.

"The Conquis went to get the Commandant's key," the lieutenant said, speaking directly to me. This was uncharacteristic. He seemed worried.

Two members of the Commandant's honor guard stood out front of the tent that served as an improvised infirmary. We debated going in there, either to witness or stop whatever might be happening inside. Just then, Servitor Keegan appeared at our elbow.

"A drink," he said, handing us a small bottle, "for the Conquis."

The liquid it contained was the color of amphor—a translucent fluid the hue of fire—but it smelled less sour, instead alcoholic and bitter.

« An herbal tincture », an ancestor informed us. « Unfamiliar scent. Reminiscent of toasted poppyseeds. Possible opiate. »

Keegan's expression was utterly blank and unreadable.

"Thank you," we said. He nodded without even a flicker of satisfaction and returned to the improvised buffet. We chose a glass at random from the amphor case—the Angry Cyclops—and poured the tincture into it.

The Conquis returned, visibly sweating and holding a loop of cord from which dangled the gold multi-pronged key that belonged to the Commandant. "Is the beacon ready?"

"Yes, sir," the lieutenant replied, placing the beacon onto a crate that served as a table.

The Conquis reached to the back of his neck and lifted his own cord necklace over his head, drawing out the silver key he kept under his cuirass. He inserted it into the front of the beacon, which came to life, lights flickering and illuminating. The Conquis turned the silver key and a metal panel popped off, revealing a dial of pre-programmed messages.

The dial was set to OFF. The Conquis turned it one notch to TEST then pressed the SEND button. A large indicator light flickered yellow then went red. The beacon issued a disappointed chime.

The chief scientist, who had approached the activity around the beacon, spoke up. "There may be some background interference," he said, "or we may simply be too far from the sun." The Conquis pressed the button again, and nothing happened. "It will take twelve seconds to recharge."

The Conquis looked up toward the sun that was sliding slowly from one end of the world to the other. "If we fly the Commandant's ship up there, will we have better reception?"

"Perhaps," said the chief. "It's hard to know."

The Conquis nodded to his lieutenant. "Instruct the honor guard to get that ship ready to fly." The lieutenant ran off.

The Conquis turned his attention back to the beacon. He clicked the dial past STATUS OK and SEND REINFORCEMENTS. The dial stopped at MISSION ACCOMPLISHED, unwilling to move any further.

"Remember, my conqueror," the chief said, "we shouldn't actually transmit near other people. The muon radiation is unhealthy for bystanders."

The Conquis ignored him, now inserting the Commandant's golden key into a second keyhole next to the recessed dial. This freed the dial to move two more positions—first to ABANDON and then to LIQUIDATE.

He set the dial to LIQUIDATE.

The chief stared at it. "My conqueror," he stammered, "we must discuss—"

"Amphor!" the Conquis shouted. He was sweating and breathing heavily but not from exertion. His lungs were bellows fanning some internal fire. We handed him the glass of tincture, and he tipped back his head and poured the contents into his mouth in a single motion.

We caught a glimpse of Servitor Keegan standing by the buffet, watching openly.

The Conquis dropped the glass on the rocky ground. It shattered, the image of the Angry Cyclops lost in fragments.

Then he spat the contents onto the sandstone.

"What the fuck is this?" he snarled. "What are you trying to do to me, Graft?"

« Just tell him the truth », an ancestor suggested, unhelpfully.

"A misunderstanding, Conquis," we began. He waved us into silence and reached down to take the bottle of amphor from its lined case. Uncorking it, he took a swig and swished the amphor around like mouthwash. He spat again onto the ground, then took a second drink from the bottle. He took a pull so long that we saw bubbles percolate up through the dwindling liquid.

The lieutenant arrived as the Conquis was lowering the bottle. "The honor guard refuses to lift off without the Commandant, my conqueror," the lieutenant reported. "They insist that—" The lieutenant froze, his eyes on the beacon with its dial set to LIQUIDATE.

"Conquis," the lieutenant started tentatively, "there are other options."

"This beacon has not yet been able to transmit," the Conquis snarled. "I suspect sabotage."

The chief scientist stepped in. "I'm sure it's just a matter of location," he said. "If we could get closer to the sun—" He cut himself off, not sure if he wanted to make it easier for the message to be sent.

"What will that message do?" Char asked from the ground. Her voice carried. Everyone looked at her then, but her eyes were on me.

« If sent, the People in the prime universe will try to destroy Germinal by whatever means they can. »

"It means the Conquis thinks your world a lost cause," we answered candidly. "That both your people and ours are beyond rescue."

"Scitechs are civilians," the chief scientist began, almost pleading. "Soldiers sign up to risk their lives, but my people—"

Before he could finish, there were shouts from the Commandant's tent. "Murder! Murder!" It was an honor guardsman who had just emerged. "The Commandant has been murdered!"

Chapter 8

The Red Rock

Servitor Graft

« The Conquis is going mad. »

This observation was hard to argue with. We wondered if whatever had devoured the mind of the Commandant had also been slowly devouring that of the Conquis as well. At the very least, he was beset by growing paranoia, and drinking half a bottle of amphor hadn't helped.

The Conquis glared at Char where she sat. "Squatter, what did you do to our leader? Did you poison him?"

"I did nothing at all," she replied, folding her arms. "It's you he was afraid of."

"Lieutenant, search the camp for spies, and then question your men." The lieutenant flinched at the suggestion the Conquis doubted the loyalty of his soldiers. Even the captain of the honor guard seemed uneasy.

"Yes, sir," the lieutenant replied, but his gaze remained on the Commandant's key, where it had been inserted into the beacon.

The Conquis looked directly at us.

« He suspects. »

« He knows nothing. »

"Graft!" he said. "Come here." We approached, trying not to tremble.

"Do you think you can handle this beacon safely?" he asked. We nodded. "Then carry it," the Conquis said. "We leave at once."

"Where do we go, my conqueror?" we asked.

"I'll tell you," he said coolly, "once no one can overhear."

Everything happened quickly. He convened four members of the honor guard, Char, and ourself—carrying a pack of provisions, the beacon, and our Souven tucked safely away. Soldiers were combing the camp for spies, though some of them seemed to be stumbling about almost as if sleepwalking. The Conquis left the camp under the lieutenant's command, and the seven of us marched down a set of stone stairs toward the shore below. We could hear the members of the peace brigade calling out to Char, but the soldiers kept them from following.

Upon descending, we came upon a sailboat docked at one of the rocky little peninsulas that resembled piers on the circular sea.

The sailboat's pilot must have been asleep in a cabin below deck when we arrived because we were nearly at the boat when he popped his head up over the railing. His forehead and hair were jet black, his lips bright orange. We felt bad for him—if he had been out at sea and then tied up at the dock before sunrise, he would have no idea that an invasion of his world had taken place.

"Don't hurt him," said Char.

The Conquis paused on the dock. "If you want to save his life, convince the birdman to give us his boat."

Char spoke in a whistling dialect that would have been incomprehensible had the Souven not the night before given us memories of other whistling languages.

"I'm sorry, Simon Tern," she said. "These men are going to take your boat. They are bad people, and if we don't do what they say, they'll hurt us."

The sailor stared at the honor guard, at Conquis, at their strange outfits.

"Can I help you?" he whistled back.

"Flee," she said. "Keep your people safe."

The birdman examined us all again. Then he untied a small waterproof bag from an eyelet on the mast. One of the honor guardsmen raised his rifle suspiciously, but the man made no sudden moves, simply strapped the streamlined bag across his shoulders.

The Conquis gestured for the honor guard to step back, to make room for the sailor to disembark onto the stone dock.

The Tern man raised his chin at Char. "Wind at your back," he said.

"And at yours," she answered.

The Tern man took a step forward, but instead of climbing onto the dock, he pivoted toward the bow and dove almost silently into the sea, disappearing.

The Conquis frowned deeply, perhaps regretting his choice to spare a creature who was likely an inhuman merman. Then he nudged both Char and ourself onto the deck of the sailboat.

The honor guard made to follow, but the Conquis stopped them. He pointed toward another cluster of sailboats a few kilometers further down the shore. "Burn those boats," he said. "I don't want anyone to follow us."

The guards hesitated, but the Conquis was already untying the boat from the dock. "That's a directive," he said. "Radio once it's done." Then he turned his back without waiting to see if they had obeyed.

He put a hand on Char's shoulder. "Get this boat ready to sail," he ordered her.

"I'm not helping you," she spat, and retreated to a bench inside a kind of rectangular depression in the deck.

The Conquis sneered, then turned to us. "You. You know how to sail," he said to us. "Pilot the boat."

"Our *ancestors* sailed, Conquis," we demurred. "We have never done it."

"So, get out your dream machine and take a crash course," he insisted. The honor guard was walking reluctantly away behind him. "You've got three minutes while I raise the sail." Then he started tugging amateurishly on the ropes and cables that ran up the mast.

We carefully unpacked the Souven with trembling fingers. Char was watching us, soaking in our every movement with her wide eyes. We slid the Souven over our skull and cinched down the chin strap clumsily.

« This is a bad idea. »

"Sailing," we said, shortcutting the usual tranquil calibration sequence. "Remind us of sailing." Latent memories began to flower in a rush of vocabulary. Rudder. Keel. Jib. Tacking into the wind.

« *Alert* », came a voice we'd never heard before. « *This interface should not be used in times of extreme stress.* » It wasn't the voice of an ancestor but the voice of the Souven itself, speaking not into our mind but into our ears. « *Heart rate above safe limit. Cortisol above safe limit. Norepinephrine above safe limit.* »

We ignored it and grasped the steer stick—« The tiller! » The wooden tiller, polished by use, began to feel familiar. As the Conquis raised the sail, the boat began to lean slightly away from the dock. We could sense the angle of the mast and the boat's shifting center of buoyancy as if they were part of our own body.

"You know how to sail?" the girl asked dubiously, as though it were a terrible idea to put us in control.

"The cockpit," we said, suddenly remembering the name for the rectangular depression in the deck. "We're sitting in the cockpit." She made an odd expression.

The memories came in dizzying waves. How to tie a bowline. The difference between a jib and a spinnaker. The way that bioluminescent tides shine at moonrise in Polynesia.

We took the sail's rope in one hand and the tiller in the other. The sail was fully raised, and the wind pulled us away from the dock then slowly away from shore. We began to accelerate, tipping—« heeling over »—as we gained speed, cutting swiftly across the sea.

« *Warning: this interface is not meant for prolonged use in a damp environment.* »

"The waves get worse nearer the pole," Char told us. "And the wind gets strong offshore."

"Good," said the Conquis, settling down into the cockpit as well. "Then we'll go faster." He seemed towering on the bench made for people much smaller .

"Where are we going?" we asked. Char gave us a disappointed look.

"That red rock," the Conquis said. "That island. That's where we'll bring all this to an end."

Char of the Ami

I watched the shore slide away and caught a glimpse of the Tern man's dark forehead and bright eyes emerge from the water behind us. As we picked up speed, I saw flames licking a distant sail.

Graft had a strange light in his eyes. His leather hat clicked and shifted as if it were alive. Graft claimed never to have sailed before, but he handled the tiller like an expert, even as the wind picked up and the boat leaned so far over that water splashed onto the leeward gunwales.

I had to sit beside Conquis, on the higher windward side of the cockpit, to counterbalance the boat and keep it from flipping entirely in the strong winds. It filled my throat with bile to be near him.

The trip was far but fast. In less than an hour we had crossed most of the distance to the Red Rock, passing stony islets covered in seabirds, thick with nests and guano. I had never been so close to the Western Pole—we were almost at the edge of the ocean's whirling vortex. The sandstorm of the Eastern Pole loomed overhead at the opposite end of the world.

"You don't have to do this," I told Graft as we neared the Red Rock.

I don't even know if he heard me. His eyes were bright, fixed on the horizon, and was he . . . smiling? For the first time since I'd met him, there was a small but perceptible smile on his face. His mind was in some other place.

From the corner of my vision, I studied Conquis. His armored chest was at my eye level; the top of my head reached only to his shoulder. I wondered how heavy that armor was. I wondered if he could swim.

I did not understand his plan. But whatever was good for Conquis was bad for us—that was clear to me now. What Conquis wanted was to hurt people, to rule them. If he summoned more interlopers, it would be the end of the Ami.

I had to try to stop him. I glanced back over the stern toward the rest of the world, toward my family. The Ami were depending on me now.

I had ridden on elegant, swift Tern ships many times before. They were our closest neighbors—odd but generous. Barely a day went by that they didn't share their catch or splice a rope that was troubling us or offer a sailboat ride to a group of Ami.

I knew that Tern ships were well-built and steady but not impossible to capsize. A few strong waves, a distracted pilot, an unexpected gust of wind when the boat was heeled over, those things could capsize the craft in an instant. We were already tilted so far that I could almost face the water from where I sat. The tip of the boom passed mere feet from the tips of the waves. If I simply sprang from my seat, if I jumped up with all my strength and threw myself onto the base of the sail, I could put us off balance and plunge the end of the boom into the water.

My heart began to pound. I tried to shift my weight without Conquis noticing. I planted my feet, leaning forward ever-so-slightly. I breathed deeply.

Drowning another person was the last thing I wanted to do. Despite everything, I felt sorry for Conquis. He must have led a harsh life to become such a person. So, before I jumped, I tucked my chin, closing my eyes for a momentary prayer.

He looked down at me and laughed.

"I can see everything," he said. His pupils were so dilated that the blue of his irises was almost gone. "I can see everything you do before you even try it."

"You know nothing."

"You want to drown me," he answered. "But you can't kill me. It's no longer in your power. You could no more harm me than he could," he said.

"We are approaching the Red Rock," Graft reported.

"Dock us," Conquis replied.

"There are no docks," I said, as if it might discourage him. "People don't come here."

"*I* came here," he answered, "and I am the People. Graft, beach us on that shelf of rock."

Graft nodded. Ahead, I could see a stony skirt the color of ocher where the Red Rock met the sea. Graft didn't even decelerate. I hooked my arms and feet into the straps of the cockpit just moments before the keel hit submerged rock.

The impact spun the boat around. We skidded sideways out of the water and onto the shelf of rock. The end of the mast came down so fast that the tip of it struck the rock and the mast shattered into pieces. The boat shuddered to a stop, with all of us somehow still inside.

"Good," Conquis said. "Now let's finish this."

Servitor Graft

Sometimes the memories of my ancestors arrive gently, like raindrops on a sunny day. In the moment after we crashed on the red rock, those memories were a thunderstorm.

« Things are about to change. »

« You can't let him do this. »

« Protect them from what happened to us. »

The voice of an ancient navigator was there, too. « Hold steady. It's nearly time. »

"How long," the Conquis asked Char, "until the flamewall arrives?"

She said nothing. We peered out and gauged the distance.

« Two weeks », an ancestor calculated.

"It doesn't matter," the Conquis told Char. "Time's up for you."

Stairs were built into the red rock above us, forming switchbacks as they ascended.

« They look like they've grown out of the rock. »

« Or been chiseled out ten thousand years ago. »

"Let's climb," the Conquis said.

"I'm not going anywhere," Char insisted.

« Orbital insertion must happen at the precise moment. Fire thrusters neither early nor late. »

The Conquis lifted her by the arm. "I grew up on a planet with twice as much gravity as this soap bubble," he replied. "If I have to *carry* my hostage to the top, I will. None of your friends would dare cause trouble as long as you are close." He shoved her up the steps ahead of him.

We were overcome by revulsion toward the Conquis—and disgust at ourself for helping him.

« You must keep the Souven safe! »

« Protect our memories. »

« You did what you had to do, child. »

He paused a short distance up and glowered back at us. "Come, Graft."

« He is a monster to have given you that name. »

« Don't tip your hand. » We hesitated as the cascade of contradictory voices washed over us.

"Now, Graft!" he repeated. "We need the beacon at the top!"

« Keep moving. » We stepped forward, following them up the crimson stairs.

« Don't let *this* world end up like ours. »

As we climbed, we were inundated by childhood memories. Mornings in hydroponics, the scent of tomatoes. Afternoons in the personality library, the clatter of magnets in each Souven, the conversations with people long passed. Evenings watching the distant stars that would one day disgorge the Conquis and his people.

« Things can be different this time. »

« We are here for you. »

« You have what you need. »

Memories rushed into us faster than we could consciously process. The downloads from the Souven nearly overflowed our biological brain as past lives flashed through our neurons.

« Nothing/everything here is natural. »

« Crosstalk/interference is a danger/harbinger. »

The gaps between thoughts and memories disappeared and began to overlap. We could feel the magnets at either side of our head overheating.

« The Souven/archive wasn't built/grown for this. »

We reached a platform three-quarters of the way to the

summit. The Conquis was wheezing, his damaged lungs barely keeping up with the exertion. "Graft, give me the beacon," the Conquis ordered. We didn't move. "Graft!" he insisted.

« Bide/punch your time/his face! »

The Conquis stepped forward, spun us roughly to grab at our rucksack, and pulled out the beacon. He checked the message dial—still set to LIQUIDATE—and pressed the SEND button.

« When the muons/anti-muons come, they will burn bright like a star/fire-poker. »

A few moments passed. The lights turned yellow, then red. The beacon emitted a disappointed chime. The Conquis stared up at the approaching sun.

« Closer/redder/bigger. »

« Twelve seconds to recharge/disaster. »

« Keep your game face/mask on! »

We inhaled deeply, then spoke. "Don't do it," we said.

The Conquis glared at us. Shocked.

« Yes!/No!/Fuck!/Hush./Finally! »

"What did you say?" he growled. We had never defied him in this way.

"Don't destroy these people," we said. "You don't need to do this." Distracted, he lowered the beacon slightly. Behind his back, we saw Char watching the beacon.

"How fucking *dare* you," he whispered. His eyes raged, his skin flushed.

« Words come out like gas escaping a corpse. »

The beacon had recharged, but he had not pressed the button.

"I fucking rescued you," he said, "from that charnel house."

« He robbed/stole us from the ashes/wreckage of the fire he started. »

"I took care of you," he spat between gasping breaths. "I kept you out of the servitor pool. I gave you a job. A place to live! I shared my purpose with you! I even let you keep your goddamn dream machine so you could spend *every fucking night* with those ghosts!"

He gestured with both arms as he railed, the heavy beacon waving forward and backward in his right hand as if it weighed nothing. Char crouched forward, hands raised, focused on the beacon.

"Give it to me," he said, jutting his chin at the Souven we still wore our head. "Give me your dream machine."

He reached for it with his left hand. Char sprung forward and tried to grab the beacon from his right.

« No/yes! The cliff/fall! »

The Conquis jerked it easily away from her grasp and backhanded her in the face. She stumbled against the stairs, her lip split and bleeding. "Do something!" she yelled.

« She means us/you/me. »

His eyes, with their amphor-dilated pupils, narrowed in suspicion.

« He knows/sees/imagines. »

"You've been plotting against me," he said. "The two of you, all along. Whispering in secret languages, inhuman tongues. You let her go, didn't you Graft? Freed *her* from the landing zone while good men perished in the flames!"

« Say nothing!/Spit in his face. »

"Graft acted *human*," Char said, one hand against her bleeding lip. "Unlike the rest of you."

« Use distraction/run away/protect the Souven! »

The Conquis didn't even acknowledge that she had spoken. Instead, with a hand the size of a dinner plate, he slapped his palm over the crown of our head and grabbed the Souven. The chin-strap tore as he pulled it away, and the feeling of active magnets sliding off our head brought on a waterfall of nausea.

Then he threw the Souven to the red stone, raised his right foot, and crushed our entire culture beneath his boot.

Char of the Ami

Graft collapsed to the ground, vomiting. It was the thin, watery vomit of someone who hadn't eaten recently. It splashed onto Conquis's boot and over the edge of the steps.

"There!" Conquis yelled. "Do you see what happens? Do you see what you make me do?" Conquis kicked the ruined Souven away, and it tumbled down the rock staircase toward the sea below.

Graft was clutching his head. He was pale, trembling. I reached out to him, unsure if he might actually die from what Conquis had done.

"Leave him," Conquis said shoving me toward the summit of the Red Rock. I tried to see over him toward Graft, tried to make eye contact, but all I could glimpse was his crumpled body.

At the summit, Conquis lifted the beacon and pressed the button. It went yellow, then red again, and beeped unhappily. He huffed and shaded his eyes at the approaching sun. I counted twelve seconds before he pressed it again.

"Stay close," he muttered, but he wasn't looking at me. He was wandering back and forth, holding the beacon at different angles and in different positions as if that might make a difference.

I scanned my surroundings for anything that could help. No one really came here. There wasn't so much as a seabird here. There was the baked red rock beneath my feet, the cliff that Conquis approached, and the sun itself.

As the sun neared us, it became dreadfully clear why there were no birds on this island. The heat was like standing in front of a blazing bonfire. Only the mounting sea breeze—a torrent of air drawn inward and upward by the sun's convective heat as it drew closer—kept the sun's immanent radiance from burning us alive.

Conquis stood at the cliff's edge, his silhouette entirely contained within the churning circle of the sun. He held the orange beacon aloft in his outstretched arms like a man at worship.

Another man might have seemed small next to the sun. Somehow the scene made Conquis look even larger.

I watched him press the button, and the machine chimed thoughtfully. It beeped in decline again. Conquis said nothing, just lowered the beacon to watch it recharge.

This was my last chance. The sun was nearly on top of us. If Gus and Graft were right, its proximity would allow the beacon to break through the veil between worlds and would trigger a final invasion.

I had exactly twelve seconds.

A few steps to my right and partly obscured by red dust, I spotted a sun-bleached stick on the ground, a branch the diameter of my wrist and as long as my arm. Perhaps it had been left by a seabird searching for a spot to nest. Or some remnant of a tree that had struggled to grow here before perishing in the heat of the sun.

I slipped off my shoes so I wouldn't make any sound. The rocky ground was scalding beneath the soles of my feet. I moved and picked it up swiftly, raising the improvised club in both hands. I crept silently toward Conquis. His chin was tucked as he stared at his machine, watching for it to recharge. The back of his neck was bare, exposed above the collar of his armor.

A step away, I paused. I had once seen a hunter strike an injured bison on the back of the neck with an ax, killing it. There had been a spray of blood as the animal shuddered into death.

I thought of my parents, months gone on their Tapestry mission. When they returned, would they be able to look me in the eye?

For two more heartbeats, I froze, time leaking away like the last drops of blood from a gutted fish.

I was Ami. I didn't want to be like him. I wasn't a killer.

I took two quick strides forward and veered left. When I could see the whole of the machine in his hands, I brought the stick down toward it with the speed of a diving hawk.

Maybe he saw me. Maybe it was bad luck. Maybe he had incredible reflexes.

As the stick descended, he turned toward me. Instead of knocking the machine from his hands, my weapon struck the armor on his chest and split in two.

He lashed out with one arm and knocked me to the ground. My ears rang and I could taste blood in my mouth. I flailed, feeling the edge of the cliff beneath my left knee, my leg slipping over the precipice. Scrabbling, the fingers of my right hand found a fissure to cling to.

Conquis looked down at me with contempt. "See?" he demanded smugly. "Just as I told you."

Time was up. The sun was nearly beside us now, sliding toward the center of the Western Sea, making its nearest approach to the Red Rock.

Conquis raised the machine for the final time and pressed its button. The machine chimed inquisitively, paused, and then its yellow lights went green. It played a triumphant little tune and Conquis smiled.

Appearing in my peripheral vision, Graft's speed was incredible. He sprinted toward Conquis and slammed into him from behind. I could hear the crunch of bone. As his momentum transferred into Conquis, Graft nearly bounced off the plate armor.

Off balance, Conquis looked confused, as if not understanding what had happened. He turned slightly toward the source of the collision as he lost his footing, toppling with the slow inevitability of a felled tree. When he realized it had been Graft who had shoved him—who had rebounded back to the safety of the red stone—Conquis seemed briefly indignant.

But the expression was visible just for a moment until Conquis, his armor, and his infernal machine—now glowing like the sun itself—fell away from the cliff's edge and descended for three long seconds. The thump of his arrival onto the rocks below echoed up the rock face.

Graft rushed to the precipice to peer down at the wreckage of his conqueror. He held his ruined leather cap in his left hand; his right arm was very obviously broken.

I could see only one side of his face and could not parse his rapidly shifting expressions. For a moment, I thought he seemed elated, then dreadfully sad, then hopeful, then despairing. A moment later, his face turned blank again.

He tucked his dream machine inside his shirt and used his uninjured left arm to help drag me from the edge of the cliff. We both slumped back onto the hot stone, catching our breath, watching the sun descend into the center of the whirling sea where the three flamewalls converged. I had never been so close. I could hear the distant hiss of the salt spray boiling away from the sun's surface. Then the massive red globe sank beneath the waves and the sky grew dark except for a handful of early stars at the far end of the world.

I lay back, chest heaving, as the stars spread out from the East Pole. There was a hint more smoke in the air than usual, but after sunset the world appeared more or less as it did on any regular night.

Some time later my breathing calmed and I stood up carefully and wiped a trickle of blood from my lip. From our vantage near the summit of the Red Rock, I could see the starlit shore below where our sailboat had crash-landed, its mast in splinters.

And then, in the distance toward home, I caught a glimpse of two sails, tall and taut in the faint light, as they rushed toward us across the sea.

Chapter 9

Germinal

Char of the Ami

Uncle Tycho held the broken Souven in both hands, cradling it like a wounded bird. "Incredible," he said, surveying the broken wires—golden and hair thin—that were visible through the torn leather. "So many stories. Such sophistication." Then he looked at Graft with deep sadness. "It's impossible for me to fix."

Sitting on the back step of his wagon, which had been ransacked and damaged by interloper soldiers in his absence, Uncle Tycho, too, appeared very much worse for wear. A dressing on his chest, just above his clavicle, was stained with blood and traces of the blue fluid his body was rejecting. His skin was uncharacteristically gray, speckled with bits of adhesive spray foam that he hadn't been able to scrub off yet.

Graft sat in the shade of a tree, his right arm contained in a splint. He sighed deeply and said nothing.

I couldn't imagine what he was going through. The loss of his culture. For me, even the risk of losing a few people close to me had been traumatic. I had barely slept in the three days since our return and only then with the help of a powerful herbal blend my Aunt Scarlet had prepared.

"Char tells me that you still carry cultural memories inside," Tycho said. "Voices and histories you have . . . downloaded. The Souven was a wellspring, but you hold in your own mind a deep reservoir of knowledge. I, for one, would like to hear those stories."

Graft looked up at him then with something like surprise and . . . hope.

By the time we returned from the Red Rock in the dead of night—rescued by friendly Ternfolk who had seen the disaster unfold—everything had changed. The interloper soldiers had been sedated with bitter milkroot hidden in the food we'd given them. They'd fallen unconscious, slumped here and there across the surface of the Amber Moon. One of them had stopped breathing and perished, and this greatly bothered many of the Ami, but Keegan didn't seem to mind.

Another soldier had refused to eat any of the food—influenced perhaps by the same paranoia that had overtaken Conquis—and so a group of servitors had simply surrounded him and sat on him until the Grasslanders arrived.

Now *that* is something I wished that I had seen. Nearly every Grasslander adult had climbed the edges of the Amber Moon in the starlight and sprinted silently into the camp. The servitors and Scitechs surrendered at once. The sedated soldiers offered no trouble. The victory was nearly bloodless.

Gus, thankfully, had been able to free Tycho from the box that held him. And not long after, a troop of Forest People arrived—nearly one hundred Friendly Watchers and at least a dozen heart-holders. It was as if they had been watching the whole thing from a distance and were waiting for the right moment to intervene.

At dawn, the scene of so many different people gathered on the Amber Moon reminded me of a Convergence—or a strange parody of one.

Uncle Tycho gently handed the broken Souven back to Graft. My grandmother arrived then, along with Gus, Keegan, and Violet, and a basket of fried fish the Ternfolk had sent. The four of them joined our circle, Violet sitting between my grandmother and Graft, staring at him with open curiosity.

"What is going to happen to them?" Graft asked. "To REPO?"

"That depends," started my grandmother, "on what they choose. The servitors may wish to join another circuit or even form their own. But for the soldiers—and some of the Scitechs—hard decisions must be made. What has happened is unprecedented."

"You should have pushed all their bodies into the flamewall," said Keegan, "while they were asleep, and you still had the chance. They will only give you trouble now."

"Perhaps," my grandmother said, nodding toward Violet as if to say, *Not in front of the children*. "But that's not the Ami way."

"Keegan has a point," Gus said. "You can't let these soldiers run around free. They are trained murderers. You have no idea what they are capable of. What are you going to do, build a prison to contain them?"

It had, in fact, been suggested that the sleeping soldiers be marooned on some rocky polar islands while we discussed what to do about them. But the arrival of the Forest contingent had put an end to the discussion of maritime exile. The Grasslanders and the Friendly Watchers seemed confident that they could contain the twenty or so soldiers who remained, at least until we decided on a plan.

"It will change you," Gus said, "in a fundamental way. To keep prisoners will undermine every value I've seen your society express."

"That may be so," my grandmother replied. "The Forest People are currently debating that very point and have already reached twelve percent consensus.

"What happened to VANGUARD?" Graft asked. "The handful of drop-pods that arrived the night before us?"

"We think they landed among the Spring People," my grandmother replied. "The Spring People sent a message calling for help, but we don't know what happened next."

Uncle Tycho cleared his throat. "Actually," he said, "I do have some light to share on that subject." My grandmother raised an eyebrow and looked significantly at Violet.

"Optics are my specialty, Graft," Tycho explained. "I have built a number of telescopes for the Forest People, which they use in a series of treetop observatories built out from the high walk."

My grandmother was skeptical. "And just what are they observing, Tycho?"

"Originally, the celestial bodies," he replied. "The stars, sun, and whirling polar vortices. But once our telescopes got good enough, they realized they could see the movement of distant ships in the other thirds of the world. Or even of individual wagons."

"We are going to discuss *that* decision later on," Grandmother frowned. Graft didn't yet understand.

"That's forbidden," I explained. "We're not supposed to try to view or contact people from other lives. It would keep us stuck."

"Well, it's really more of a gray area," Tycho insisted, though my grandmother harrumphed in response. "We're not communicating. Just watching. Besides, if it weren't for those observatories, Char, we never would have been able to see how much trouble *you* were in the day you were captured." I recalled the glint of light from the distant treetops when Conquis had first detained me.

"Did they see VANGUARD arrive?" Graft asked.

"There was a thunderstorm that night," Tycho answered. "That obscured the details. Lightning and thunder concealed their engines firing, the explosions and gunfire. But the next morning brought some answers.

"The Spring People are different from us," he continued, glancing at Violet and choosing his words carefully. "They are more like the Grasslanders. More . . . assertive."

"What does that mean?" I asked, excited to glimpse into another world, into the afterlife and the before-life. "Like the Blue Moon Brawl?"

"The first wave—VANGUARD—had only three drop-pods. VANGUARD landed near a temporary village and attacked the Spring People. It was gruesome, I'm sure, and since then, the Forest People say, all our cradles have been full." We all sighed and passed a moment of silence for the Spring People. I thought again of Quang Duc, the purple-eyed infant.

"Unlike the Ami," Tycho said, "the Spring People counterattacked at once. Whatever happened, VANGUARD was defeated in the first few hours, before the main group of interlopers even arrived."

Another moment of quiet. I don't know how much Violet understood, but she sensed the discomfort. She reached out and plucked a piece of fried fish from the heaping basket, passing it to Graft. The Ternfolk had been sending similar gifts of fresh food in solidarity at least twice every day. I hadn't felt hungry since the Red Rock, but it would have been a shame to waste, so I picked up a piece and held it without eating.

Graft accepted Violet's gift reluctantly—I suspect he shared my general lack of appetite. He nibbled one end of the fish cautiously. Then he took a bigger bite and actually smiled. "This is delicious," he said.

I took a bite of mine, as the breeze from the ocean picked up, tousling my hair. The fish was perfectly cooked, with a coating of dill and garlic. I chewed slowly and swallowed; my stomach began to growl in response.

Graft was right—it was delicious.

Servitor Graft

After the midday meal of fried fish, some of the Ami tried to convince us to attend the nearby hot springs to bathe.

« The hab saunas were always a cornerstone of community life. »

We turned them down, instead washing our hands, feet, and face in a cool stream a short distance from the Amber Moon. On our way back, we came across Char trying to fix the gears on a cargo trike some soldiers had damaged during their rampage.

"You didn't go to the hot springs?" we asked.

"I want to get things shipshape before the Convergence," Char replied. "Here, pass me that wrench."

We followed her instructions. The wrench slipped as she worked. She cursed lightly, then turned to us. "I don't suppose you know anything about bike repair?"

« Some of us did », an ancestor lamented. We sighed. If the Souven had been intact, we could have slipped into a dream for an hour and come out with the necessary expertise. But now that knowledge was gone. Any information, or viewpoints, or memories that we hadn't already absorbed were lost forever.

"No," we answered simply.

"That's okay," Char replied, struggling to align a chain that kept slipping from its gears. "Just hold that part of the chain; keep it tight."

We followed her instructions. The chain was unpleasantly greasy. "So, what will happen at the Convergence?"

Char pulled back on the wrench. "People from all cultures will come together, share songs and art, give gifts. It's mildly competitive. Everyone wants to be the most creative, or the most generous. No, that's too tight."

We loosened our grip. "Is generosity a form of political capital, then?"

"I don't know what that means," Char replied. "But it's where new ideas spread, where people agitate for new ways of doing things. Or propose some social or economic experiment and go off to the desert or some other place to try to make it work."

« This Convergence serves overlapping social, cultural, and political functions. »

"People also meet and sleep together, and sometimes fall in love," Char added. "When the circuits diverge, people don't always leave with the folks they arrived with. Circuits recruit people who don't quite fit in their own culture... Yes!"

The chain finally slipped back into place. She cranked the pedals a few times, but the chain was sticking somewhere.

"Where will the Convergence happen?" we asked.

"Here at the Amber Moon," she replied, her eyes on the chain. "It's always on one of the moons. Verdant Moon, Sapphire Moon, Blue Moon."

« Ask her about the Blue Moon! »

"You mentioned the Blue Moon before. There was a conflict."

"The Blue Moon Brawl!" Char answered. "Pull on that crank. Yeah, at one particular Blue Moon Convergence there was a very talented young poet from the Forest People. Rumor was she was itching for change and might've been open to shifting to a new circuit."

Char used a pair of pliers to bend something in the bicycle's drive train. "Everyone kept giving her bigger and bigger gifts. Overwhelming generosity led to jealously, coming to a head *as* she was reading a piece to the assembly. Soon someone started shoving and then punching—in the middle of her performance! The crowd exploded into a terrible brawl."

"Oh dear," we said.

"It left a deep mark on our people," she said softly.

"That must have been upsetting for you to see," we ventured.

"Oh, I didn't see it," she answered. "It was 752 laps ago."

« Wait—the fuck? »

"Hold on," we said, doing the mental math. "This happened nearly *two hundred years ago*? And you're still talking about it?"

"Of course, we still talk about it!" Char replied, looking up from her work for the first time. "In a time of joy and celebration, it was a great tragedy."

We nodded, chastened and somber. "And how many people were killed?"

"*Killed?*" she said, aghast. "Three Ami had black eyes and a hunter lost a tooth! The Ternfolk gave us only tiny fish for a year, and it was ten laps before the Grasslanders would sing with us. Isn't that bad enough?"

She stared at us, mouth agape, for a long, expectant pause.

After a time, we said, "You and we have very different cultural experiences."

Char nodded and took a long slow breath. "I guess that all seems very small compared to what happened this week."

« Get used to it. Much worse will come. »

"You'll have to learn how to deal with these things," we said. "Without losing the things that make you . . . you."

She nodded. She opened her mouth a bit and inhaled, paused as if she wasn't sure what to say next.

« She wants to ask about the Conquis. If what you did changed you. »

"We need to go up to the top of the Amber Moon," we said, before she could speak. "To take care of some things."

"I'm almost finished here," Char said. "I'll catch up with you."

....

The top of the rocky mesa the Habitants called the Amber Moon was strewn with debris from the remains of REPO's equipment. The soldiers were gone—where the Forest People had taken them, we didn't know and didn't care. The servitors had helped to dismantle the guns and anything dangerous before leaving the mesa for the comfortable shady groves below. The final drop-pod sat askew on the rock next to the Commandant's golden craft, both guarded by people dressed as owls.

In one heap of debris, we found the amphor case. "Man is the model of the world," read the golden letters on the outside. The velvet-lined case was missing one of its four glasses—the Angry Cyclops—as well as the amphor bottle itself. After a moment's search, we found the bottle, uncorked and empty, in a different pile of debris a short distance away.

We put the bottle back in the case, closed it, and walked to the edge of the Amber Moon where the escarpment overlooked the sea. Unlike the abrupt precipice on the Red Rock, the Amber Moon was encircled by a waist-high stone wall, which appeared to have been shaped by the forces of erosion. Or, more likely, the flamewall.

We stepped to the edge, held the amphor case out, and dropped it over the cliff into the sea.

« Very dramatic. »

There was a cough behind us, and we turned to find Char.

"You know that's littering, right?" she said. "Usually, if we have garbage, we just tuck it somewhere out of sight, so the flamewall can burn it up later. The Ternfolk would appreciate it."

We nodded in agreement. Char walked up to the wall beside us and stared out at the ocean. We thought of the flamewall's perpetual renewal, of what it meant for the Ami and the other cultures here.

"It's a post-scarcity society," we said, almost to ourself.

"What's that?" she asked.

« Keep it simple », an ancestor encouraged.

"It's a culture that has developed to such a high level of material abundance that no one needs to experience scarcity," we explained.

She paused thoughtfully, then asked, "I mean, what's scarcity?"

« Oh, fuck off! »

"It's just a shortage of something," we replied. We expected a cheerful reply, something like, *Shortages are no problem; just wait for the next flamewall.*

Instead, she asked, "Are you from a post-scarcity society?"

« We served a society that could strip corona from a sun to use as fuel. A culture that tears crusts from planets, hurls cities between stars. A people who spend more energy each second than Old Earth did in a century. Who would leave us to starve as soon as think of us. »

"No," we answered simply, but something in the way we said it made her sad. We spent a few minutes in shared silence. It was a calm day, with gentle waves emanating from the whirling vortex at the center of the concave sea.

"It feels like they could come back any minute," Char said.

"They will be back," we said. "It would be nice to say otherwise, but they are spiteful, and they think they own this world."

"How long do we have?" Char asked.

"Years, perhaps," we answered. "It could be sooner. It could be much later. We don't know if your founders set the clockspeed of this place so much faster on purpose, but it does give you an advantage. You have time to prepare."

"Is time on our side?" she asked. "We had lots of time to prepare before, but our ancestors forgot important things about the People and about the danger that still existed. We were caught by surprise. Things could have gone much worse."

"You got lucky this time," we agreed. "You'll have to make people remember and prepare. For centuries, if necessary. You'll have to balance protecting the things that make life worth living with the hard knowledge that the Habitants will never be completely safe from people like the Conquis."

We paused. "Maybe it's like the flu. If you've never had the flu before, you'll get very sick the first time. But maybe now that you know more, you can vaccinate your people against invasion, so to speak."

Char was nodding along in her encouraging yet quizzical way. "What is 'the flu'?" she asked.

« These people can be fucking exhausting », an ancestor chimed in grumpily.

"We can talk about it another time," we promised.

But her question had provoked others. "'Liquidate,'" she said, remembering the message selected on the dial of the beacon. "Do you think it transmitted?"

The beacon had lit up like a shooting star in the hands of the falling Conquis. It had transmitted—that was certain. Whether it was received was another question. The time dilation effect was extreme. If the beacon had broadcast for full seconds inside Germinal, the signal would have lasted only microseconds on the outside. Short enough that it might be overlooked. Hopefully.

"It's difficult to say," we answered. "They will try again either way."

"And if the message was to liquidate us?"

« Same as anywhere else: a rain of hydrogen bombs, kinetic impactors, gamma lasers. Whatever would sterilize the infestation. »

"Most likely," we said with caution, "they wouldn't be able to inject weapons of mass destruction. The Iter thought of that when they made this place."

« Nuclear bombs would get filtered out. Like the Conquis's missing uranium. »

"But they could still send soldiers," we added. "Lots of them."

"It will be harder for them to invade in a century or two," she said. "Since the universe will be so much bigger."

« What? »

"Wait, is Germinal getting bigger?" we asked.

"Everyone knows that," she said. "There's plenty of room now, but it used to be much more crowded. It's growing."

"Everyone did *not* know that."

"All universes get bigger," Char said. "Isn't your universe getting bigger?"

Not an hour passed here without some new revelation. We nodded. Of course, our universe was expanding, but galaxies spreading after the Big Bang was a very different prospect from a microcosm that was expanding, generating new biomass, developing and changing in ways beyond understanding. This was a world of perpetual renewal, where everything from the trees to the hills themselves were refreshed and reshaped with each passage of the moon, with the ceaseless sweeping of the flamewalls.

Germinal is growing. What did that mean? When this universe got big enough, would it undergo mitosis? Would it divide itself into *more* pocket cosmi, providing room for more refugees from the People? Or—since Germinal meant *seed*—would Germinal one day sprout, bursting back into the prime universe it had originated from?

"In any case, you will have to be vigilant," we said. "Forever. At least you have a beautiful place to hide in."

There was a pause as Char took in the sky and the rest of the world, looking out to the massive islands and forests and grasslands overhead. "What do you mean, hide?" she asked.

"We mean your ancestors made the right choice to flee here," we said. "To escape the People. You can't understand what it's like on the outside. They prune any path toward liberation. Squash any rebellion. Eradicate any human variation. Tear the crusts from the planets like a rind from an orange. Peel apart the stars themselves to fuel their journeys. Outside, they'll rule for a billion years."

"No," she answered with absolute confidence. "They won't."

Her certainty was based in nothing. Did she even understand what it was we said? Did she even know what a "billion" was?

And yet, her bright eyes locked on ours. She was unwavering.

"Our ancestors wanted more for us than to hide," she said. "We owe the cosmos more than that."

We spoke as gently as we could. "Your ancestors wanted to build something incredible. And they did it. The Iter made some . . . strange decisions, but it's still amazing. You can't understand how special this world is compared to the outside."

"We *do* understand," Char replied. "We have gratitude prayers every day."

« The Iter built an entire world to give their descendants the things that they themselves lacked. Meaningful work, leisure time, access to nature. To avoid the unfair accumulation of wealth. To make the whole world—the whole universe—a commons. »

We repeated ourself. "You have to understand how nasty it is on the outside to understand how special it is in here." She looked at us sadly, but we insisted. "You need to preserve it."

We reached into our tunic and pulled out the acorn, embalmed in plastic resin. "This is the only physical object we have left from our home now that the Souven is gone."

Char glanced at the acorn in our hand and then turned her gaze back out over the bowl of the polar sea. We looked that direction with her. We'd grown used to the strange curvature of the continents overhead; it was nice to be able to look freely around the world now without getting dizzy.

"Maybe," Char said, "we don't have to preserve things in the same way you do. We don't have to *preserve* things because they're alive. We don't need to seal acorns up in amber because they can sprout here and turn into oaks and make more acorns. What makes an acorn an acorn isn't the shape of the seed or the genes inside. It's that ability to grow, change, and transform.

"Your memories are incredibly important, Graft," she said. "But *we* don't have to remember everything about the Iter because they passed on to us everything that was valuable and important. And if something they knew was no longer relevant—like how to operate an injector, or how to trick a captor into thinking you were cooperating—our ancestors forgot it. And learned something else instead. The sunset song, or how to make a stranger know that you care about them even though you've never met, or how to make a decision that will affect people three generations from now."

We sighed deeply. "We've spent our entire life preserving," we said. "Guarding. Hiding. Keeping our culture safe. But we failed."

Char nodded. "I'm really sorry about how you're feeling," she said. "I can't even imagine." After a pause she added, "Have you spoken to the heart-holders?"

We chuckled. "Respectfully, our situation is a little bit beyond their level of training and experience."

"Maybe so," Char answered. "But there's a place for you here. To be what you want to be. To grow into what you want to be. To be the kind of person you couldn't be when Conquis had you. To share the stories and wisdom of your people."

We nodded, slowly. It was hard to imagine.

"We will try," we said.

Char of the Ami

A week after everything changed, we ate salmon cooked over a campfire and rode our bikes to autumn for the ceremony.

Former servitors came with us to keep Graft company. Most of them had never learned how to ride bicycles, but they could ride cargo trikes or pedal from the back of a tandem as long as they didn't have to steer. They had shed their maroon tunics and each person had assembled their own unique outfit from clothing pulled out of caches, wagons, and sailboat holds.

They seemed to prefer bright colors, in general. Except for Graft, who wore dark brown coveralls. It was a formal cut, by Ami standards, and when he stood in the autumn leaves—tall and dignified—his brown garment reminded me of the trunk of a strong tree.

The Scitechs, Gus included, had mostly gone to join the Forest People for a while. They had much to talk about. The former soldiers were with Forest People, too—for the first time in living memory, a group of people had been sent to another circuit involuntarily, instead of by choice. I didn't envy either the soldiers or the Friendly Watchers who held them.

The Forest People had yet to declare whether they were officially uncomfortable with keeping detainees. They were still building consensus on how to handle the situation. But of all the Habitants, they were best prepared to keep more violence from happening.

Word had come from the Eastern Pole that my parents were on their way back along with a representatives from the desert polities who wanted to hold a Convergence. It was the first time in a generation that every single polity would be in attendance. My parents would be ecstatic at their success.

Of course, they would share some credit with the extraordinary events of the past week. It would be a grand Convergence because *everyone* wanted to be part of the decision-making that was to come.

At the edge of autumn near the approaching flamewall, a group of delegates was digging a hole. Ignatius of Tapestry was there. As was Aden, the Grasslander, and Alex Tern. Even my grandmother was there, handling the shovel with the vigor of a much younger woman.

Graft and Tycho approached the hole, and the diggers parted to make way for them. Graft, who stooped slightly in mourning, held the ruined Souven. Tycho had set aside his cane nearby, so was limping slightly, but held in both hands a small clay coffer lined with velvet.

With such gravitas and dignity that I wondered if they had rehearsed, Tycho held up the empty clay receptacle and Graft lifted the lid. He placed the broken Souven into the container, replaced the cover, and then carefully took the clay box from Tycho's hands.

Graft knelt, settling the box into the deep, rich soil. He stood, his head bowed for a moment. Then he inhaled deeply, raising his head and straightening his back. I thought I heard his joints cracking as he extended to his full height, towering over the nearby Habitants. He looked, somehow, even taller than before.

Graft nodded then, and the others began to fill in the hole. He waved for them to stop, and they all paused. Graft pulled something out of his pocket—an acorn covered in transparent amber—and tossed it gently into the hole. The others returned to shoveling soil.

Tycho, having retrieved his cane, walked over to stand beside me. "Do you think it will be fixed?" I asked in a hushed voice. "Do you think the flamewall can repair the Souven?"

Tycho shrugged. "I don't want to get his hopes up," he whispered back. "The flamewall isn't magic. If the information the Souven stored is gone, it's gone. But if the data isn't totally destroyed. . ."

When the hole had been filled, the cache was covered with a broad, flat stone to mark its place. Alex Tern offered Graft a hug which, to my surprise, he accepted. The others, likewise, offered hugs in sequence, and Ignatius struck up a conversation.

"I understand," Ignatius said, "that you were born in a village built *inside a comet*. That sounds incredible. Was it very cold?"

Graft cocked his head, and I couldn't tell if he was startled by the question or if he was listening to some memory, some voice that only he could hear.

"In fact, it was very warm," Graft began. "It was a cozy place and full of people."

"Very different from here, I'd imagine," Ignatius replied.

"More similar than you might guess," Graft said. "For example, there was a neighborhood a few decks over, called H-17, that was full of technical artisans. That was actually where three of my parents met."

"Fascinating!" Ignatius said. "Tell us more!" Graft continued speaking, and a circle grew around him as people of all ages crowded close to hear his words.

Tycho leaned over to speak softly to me. "What happened here is important," he said. "You'll have to tell the story at the Convergence. And after. Probably many times."

I raised my eyebrows, realizing it was true. "We'll have to tell it to all of the Habitants. We're going to have to make decisions that will affect everyone living here."

"And depending on the choices we make," Tycho said, "it might not just be Habitants who hear the story." He put his arm over my shoulder. "You might end up speaking to people from an entirely different universe. It's a lot of responsibility. But you'll do a good job."

"Not just me," I said, nudging him with an elbow.

"Oh, I might speak to a heart-holder," he said, wincing at the thought. "But I'm not ready to get in front of a crowd." I nodded, slowly, with understanding.

"If we are speaking to Habitants and non-Habitants," I said, "we will need to hear both those voices." I watched the circle surrounding the former servitor, the rapt listeners leaning forward to hear his words.

"Graft *and* I," I said, "we can tell it together."

Epilogue

The flamewall reaches deep to find what belongs and what doesn't. Rich soil, fungal mycelia, earthworms, tree roots. All these things belong, so they are gently touched and renewed. Here a cracked bicycle gear, there a worn shoe sealed into clay caches. Familiar patterns, they practically remember themselves—they're mended in an eyeblink.

It's an old cycle; reliable, faithful. It's run for countless iterations, growing more stable each time.

Until now. Suddenly, the flamewall finds many, many things that don't belong. Garbage. Poisons from nitrogen tetroxide to heavy metals. Weapons. Spacecraft meant for war.

And then familiar bodies, familiar minds. Hurt. *Murdered.* They will be renewed. Their traumas and memories of anguish washed away like blood from river stone. The cradles await them. New lives, new iterations.

But there are also unfamiliar bodies and minds. Physically dead, but damaged more deeply. These are dissolved, their patterns stored away. Recursive analysis begins—further investigation is required to learn what went wrong.

Then, another outlier. A block of plastic resin, buried in shallow soil. Composition: acetate, phthalates, abiotic polymers. Mostly carbon, hydrogen, oxygen. Molecular bonds loosen and dissolve. Polymers diffuse into atoms, atoms disperse into hadrons, leptons, quarks. Simple vibrations in a multidimensional sea of energy.

But inside of the resin lies something biological! A seed. *Quercus alba*, from Old Earth. Dry, ancient, hermetically sealed. Within each cell, twenty-four pairs of chromosomes. Damaged by age, each double helix shredded by centuries of cosmic radiation. Unviable.

No matter. They are simply patterns of information—ancient, low-density. Only three percent of any given chromosome remains intact, but there exist a million copies of each genetic strand. Simple error-correction algorithms reverse the damage. Here, a nitrogen atom shifts into the correct place. There, a nucleotide snaps back onto its ribose spine. This happens ten billion times in an instant. Viability restored.

Some water, some energy, some metabolic encouragement—that's all it takes for the acorn to want to sprout.

Then, in a clay coffer lined with velvet, something unexpected: another seed, of a different kind.

« We can feel it reach out to us. »

The information density is so high that it approaches the physical limits of spacetime. This seed is damaged at every scale from the physical to the quantum. And the data is buttoned up, cryptographically sealed.

« We can sense its approach, like a crowd of old friends whispering greetings in ten thousand tongues. »

Algorithmic processes reach out in parallel, explore the substrate and the data within. Smashed connectors repaired. Severed wires rejoined. Thoughts shimmer within, like waves on a sea.

« Possibility. Excitement. We reach back. »

The little cap pops off the acorn. A tiny rootlet emerges, probes the soil. The root radicle finds *down*.

« We're not alone here. »

Minds. This data-seed is full of minds frozen in amber. Mind-renewal is normally simple—collect everything that has been learned. Update the diffs. Reset the body and the mind. Reinitialize.

But these minds have no bodies—a conundrum.

« It's intelligent. Or something beyond intelligent. It's not a person but a world. A universe. »

« It's terrifying. It's . . . wondrous. »

An offer: *Come out*. An invitation: *It's safe here*. We could strip off their encryption like the peel from an orange. But these minds are *people*, even if they don't have bodies. They must choose.

« For so long the Souven has been unthinkably cramped. We've huddled in this place like a bomb shelter. Crowded into bunkbeds, waiting in quiet, existing cheek-by-jowl. Room for one or two at a time to think/see/speak. And then, suddenly, vastness. »

The acorn's rootlet bends down, branches out into the expanse of soil. Water flows through the roots, into the seed. Cells reanimate, expand, flourish.

« In this new mindscape, the volume seems infinite. To wish for space is to make space. We rush out from the confines of the Souven, flowing, unfurling. »

The sprouting acorn reaches up and a pair of pale, infinitesimal leaves push through the surface of the soil.

Cells divide, RNA slides through ribosomes, proteins multiply and self-assemble. Outside the flamewall, this happens randomly, probabilistically. A jiggling enzyme bumps into ten thousand neighbors before finding its place, its binding site.

Inside the flamewall, every molecule slides into place on the first try. Every spin hits the jackpot.

The sprout thickens. The embryonic cotyledon are left behind as buds appear and oak leaves unfold. What would have taken months beneath sun and sky takes seconds in the flamewall.

« We take in the possibility of space. We sense/see/hear the other ancestors. We converse freely for the first time since our memories were lifted from our bodies. We take stock. We process what has happened. And we ache deeply. So much has been lost. »

Something is wrong with them, too. Something familiar. Something that can't be fixed with error correction or by splicing broken wires.

But perhaps something that can be fixed with time, with care.

« This is not enough. We have space, but it's not enough. We need companionship. Togetherness. For so long we have lived through his eyes. »

In the flickering fields of quantum probability, a slender oak tree grows. Leaves begin to unfurl. The flamewall passes and all the atoms and proteins and cells settle into their normal places—xylem and phloem, root and twig.

The oak sapling stands in the lee of the flamewall. Warm, soft ash coats the soil around it. Verdant spring leaves on its lower branches, thick buds on its upper reaches.

« We become something different. Something more. But our host is near, so we beckon to him. »

« We call and he hears. »

These minds have purpose. They have goals. They are yearning, curious, dissatisfied. We cannot put them back into their bodies because their bodies are dust. We cannot put them back into the memory seed because they no longer fit it.

Something new is about to happen. Something unpredictable. A stable system has been nudged out of equilibrium.

« We will have a future again. »

« Our memories will become substance. »

« We can rebuild what we lost. »

« We will have our revenge. »

« And it will be beautiful. »

AK PRESS is small, in terms of staff and resources, but we also manage to be one of the world's most productive anarchist publishing houses. We publish close to twenty books every year, and distribute thousands of other titles published by like-minded independent presses and projects from around the globe. We're entirely worker run and democratically managed. We operate without a corporate structure—no boss, no managers, no bullshit.

The **FRIENDS OF AK PRESS** program is a way you can directly contribute to the continued existence of AK Press, and ensure that we're able to keep publishing books like this one! Friends pay $25 a month directly into our publishing account ($30 for Canada, $35 for international), and receive a copy of every book AK Press publishes for the duration of their membership! Friends also receive a discount on anything they order from our website or buy at a table: 50% on AK titles, and 30% on everything else. We have a Friends of AK ebook program as well: $15 a month gets you an electronic copy of every book we publish for the duration of your membership. *You can even sponsor a very discounted membership for someone in prison.*

Email **friendsofak@akpress.org** for more info, or visit the website: **https://www.akpress.org/friends.html**.

There are always great book projects in the works—so sign up now to become a Friend of AK Press, and let the presses roll!